"Will you never want me, my prince?" Serena asked

"I—I..." Cade stared at her, uncertain as to how to answer. "You have to give me a minute to think this through. I don't know that I can make love to a woman intended for my brother. My mind still thinks of you that way."

Serena leaned close to him, near enough to tease him with her perfume and her femininity. "Prince Kadar, your brother did not want me."

"He didn't have a chance to find out."

"The race goes to the swiftest," she said, placing her fingers lightly over his hand. "In this case, the crown, with all its benefits and drawbacks, goes to the fastest warrior. That would be you."

"Only because Mac—"

"You are my choice," she told him sincerely. "His arranged marriage is now yours. So, my husband, do you find me desirable enough to make love to me?"

Dear Reader,

May is "*Get Caught Reading*" month, and there's no better way for Harlequin American Romance to show our support of literacy than by offering you an exhilarating month of must-read romances.

Tina Leonard delivers the next installment of the exciting Harlequin American Romance in-line continuity series TEXAS SHEIKHS with *His Arranged Marriage*. A handsome playboy poses as his identical twin and mistakenly exchanges "I do's" with a bewitching princess bride.

A beautiful rancher's search for a hired hand leads to more than she bargained for when she finds a baby on her doorstep and a *Cowboy with a Secret,* the newest title from Pamela Browning. 2001 WAYS TO WED concludes with *Kiss a Handsome Stranger* by Jacqueline Diamond. Daisy Redford's biological clock had been ticking…until a night of passion with her best friend's brother left her with a baby on the way! And in *Uncle Sarge*, a military man does diaper duty…and learns about fatherhood, family and forever-after love. Don't miss this heartwarming romance by Bonnie Gardner.

It's a terrific month for Harlequin American Romance, and we hope you'll "get caught reading" one of our great books.

Wishing you happy reading,

Melissa Jeglinski
Associate Senior Editor
Harlequin American Romance

Texas Sheikhs:
HIS ARRANGED MARRIAGE

Tina Leonard

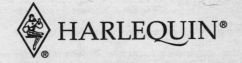

HARLEQUIN®

TORONTO • NEW YORK • LONDON
AMSTERDAM • PARIS • SYDNEY • HAMBURG
STOCKHOLM • ATHENS • TOKYO • MILAN • MADRID
PRAGUE • WARSAW • BUDAPEST • AUCKLAND

Special thanks and acknowledgment are given to
Tina Leonard for her contribution
to the Texas Sheikhs series.

This book was a gift, and I thank Melissa, Denise and Tashya for giving it to me. Lisa and Dean, Mumsie can cease being a grouch now. Olivia Holton, your treatise on "sheikh appeal" was invaluable—this jet's for you! Fatin Soufan and Shadin Quran, thanks for the support— this sheikh's for you! Last, a smile to the one who inspired me as I wrote this book. You'll never know you were the sheikh in my heroine's dreams, but that is as it should be.

RECYCLED PAPER
RECYCLED PAPER

ISBN 0-373-16873-X

HIS ARRANGED MARRIAGE

ABOUT THE AUTHOR

As a child, Tina Leonard cut her teeth on Alfred Hitchcock black-and-white TV shows, enjoying late-night summer episodes with her stepmother, Judy. To this day, Tina has an affinity for the old, scary movies, and the hokier, the better! Tina in person is a self-avowed chicken, however. The only brave thing she has ever done is scare a large rat away from an open car door! She eschews the blood-and-guts movies and books, preferring instead more psychological bogeys, and believes fervently that the most compelling part of any good romantic mystery is the timeless and magical love between a man and a woman.

Books by Tina Leonard

HARLEQUIN AMERICAN ROMANCE
748—COWBOY COOTCHIE-COO
758—DADDY'S LITTLE DARLINGS
771—THE MOST ELIGIBLE...DADDY
796—A MATCH MADE IN TEXAS
811—COWBOY BE MINE
829—SURPRISE! SURPRISE!
846—SPECIAL ORDER GROOM
873—HIS ARRANGED MARRIAGE

HARLEQUIN INTRIGUE
576—A MAN OF HONOR

Don't miss any of our special offers. Write to us at the following address for information on our newest releases.

Harlequin Reader Service
U.S.: 3010 Walden Ave., P.O. Box 1325, Buffalo, NY 14269
Canadian: P.O. Box 609, Fort Erie, Ont. L2A 5X3

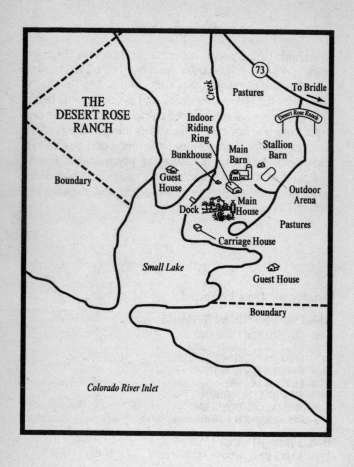

THE
DESERT ROSE
RANCH

Boundary

Creek

73

Pastures

To Bridle

Desert Rose Ranch

Indoor
Riding
Ring

Main
Barn

Stallion
Barn

Bunkhouse

Guest
House

Dock

Main
House

Outdoor
Arena

Pastures

Carriage House

Small Lake

Guest House

Boundary

Colorado River Inlet

Chapter One

"I'm not getting married," Mac Coleman stated, "and that's that."

"That would be my response," Cade Coleman agreed, shooting a grin at their mother, Rose. She stared back at her twin sons with dismay. "Mac shouldn't have to marry a woman he doesn't know—much less love—princess or otherwise."

"Cade, you know that with Alex's marriage to Hannah, Mac became the next prince in line to secure a royal match."

"It's hell being the oldest twin," Mac grumbled. "I hate to be a disappointment to the family, but I'm much better with horses than women. Besides, thirty years old is much too young to get married."

"Much," Cade responded cheerfully, lifting a glass of tea to his brother's sentiment.

"This is a serious matter, Cade," Rose insisted.

Mac snorted. "Not since it's not his neck in the matrimonial noose."

Cade clapped his brother on the back. "Don't take it so hard, bro. Maybe this princess is just what you need to break you out of your shell."

"I like my shell just fine. Look, I spend long hours with the horses. She's not going to want to be brought here and then left while I'm working. I'm pretty certain princesses expect to be waited on hand and foot."

Cade raised his brows. "Well, those twenty-three minutes that saved me from being born first are certainly playing in my favor now. I wouldn't be in your boots for anything."

"The importance of this matter can not be underlined enough." Rose leaned forward from her seat at the head of the table. "A marriage to Serena Wilson-Al Farid secures the lineage and will put the political turmoil concerning Balahar and Sorajhee to rest."

"Imagine that a simple wedding band and an 'I do' can work such miracles," Cade said. "Mac's fine here at The Desert Rose, Mother. None of us needs to marry King Zakariyya Al Farid's adopted daughter."

"It is your rightful heritage, Kadar," Rose said quietly. "It was stolen from us many years ago. This will put everything right again."

Mac shook his head as Cade began another spirited rebuttal. "Mother's right. I just need a day or two to absorb this." Prince Makin—Mac—stood, suddenly tall and imposing beside his mother. Cade watched as mother and son stared at each other for a single second. Mac nodded before leaning down to give his mother a respectful brush on the cheek.

Then he left the room.

Cade sighed as he felt Rose's even gaze upon him.

"I know. I'm not a dutiful son."

"No. You're not."

"Looks like royal duty stinks to me."

"Duty is an interchangeable word with responsibility." Rose took a sip of tea. "Mac will do what he knows is right for The Desert Rose, and he also knows he is making me very happy. It is no small thing to be able to help achieve peace between countries that desperately need it right now, either."

"Good boy, Mac," Cade said under his breath.

"Cade, you have done a fine job handling the business end of The Desert Rose operations. But it is no secret to you, I am sure, that eventually this alliance could assure our position as a foremost Arabian horse farm. The most urgent factor, however, is that we gain back the royal heritage that was wrongly wrested from the family. I feel certain your father, were he alive, would approve."

"No downside to the whole thing except for Mac's heart. He's never been easygoing or inclined to take life lightly."

"No, he lacks that particular dynamic of your personality,'' Rose agreed. ''Sometimes not an altogether bad thing.''

''He's too serious. He's reflective. He'll suffer if the marriage doesn't work out. You know Mac will blame himself, at the least because of the responsibility involved. He's a poster boy for doing the right thing. If this princess is a pampered pillow-sitter, or even if they simply can't make this union a happy one, Mac will take it hard.''

''Whereas you would simply say, 'Buck up, Princess Serena baby, this is life in Texas. Not like you saw on the *Dallas* TV show.'''

''Maybe.'' He eyed his mother from the other end of the table, recognizing the steel in her eyes and her tone.

''I agree she would find it difficult to adjust to Bridle. That's why Mac will live in Balahar for at least a year. It's important that he learn about the country for the eventual day when he takes over as ruler.''

''Does Mac know that?''

Rose shook her head. ''One shock at a time, I think.''

''It'll kill him to be away from his horses that long.'' But Cade knew that Mac would voice very little complaint. He would simply do it—for Rose. For The Desert Rose. And for a country he'd never seen.

''Oh, hell,'' he muttered. ''I've heard that heavy

is the head which wears the crown, but this is ridic-
ulous.''

"They have Arabian horses in Balahar," Rose reminded him. "No doubt Mac can learn much from
the king's stables."

Cade didn't think Mac would have a lot of time
to go through the king's stables if he was supposed
to be a devoted suitor to a princess. Mac wasn't the
kind of man who was at ease with women, parties
and idle chitchat.

On the other hand, Cade was.

He got to his feet. "I think I'll go talk to him."

"Don't try to talk Mac out of this. His mind is
made up."

Cade met his mother's eyes. "Why would I try
to do something like that?"

"Because you don't take your heritage seriously," Rose snapped in an uncharacteristically
sharp tone. "This is more important than I can make
you understand."

Cade left the room. He did take life seriously.
From the zygote that had been halved between him
and Mac, however, the talent for lightheartedness
had been unequally distributed.

Mac would never be happy in a foreign country,
playing at being a prince. His heart was at The Desert Rose. No prize princess could ever make up for
leaving that behind.

"Don't do it," Cade told Mac as he came upon his brother leaning against a wood post outside. Cade knew what Mac was staring at. Three horses, some of the world's most admired and coveted breeding stock, grazed inside the corral. Mac's eyes may have been on the Arabian horses, but Cade knew his heart was tearing at the thought that a bride would soon take precedence. "I told Mother I wouldn't try to talk you out of anything, but I just want to remind you that you haven't officially agreed yet. You don't have to marry anyone you don't want to."

Mac snorted. "Don't you think I know that? But I could do it. I mean, what would it hurt? I don't have time to hunt for a wife. I'm not the world's luckiest guy when it comes to relationships and picking women. The bright side of this is that the princess won't expect a whole lot out of me if she's been groomed for an arranged marriage."

"So why look a gift horse in the mouth? Is that what you're saying?"

Mac smiled wryly. "So to speak."

"Maybe Serena's throwing a fit about having to marry you."

"I've thought about that. She may have to do it, but no doubt she's not exactly jumping up and down." He sighed. "That doesn't make me feel much better, to be honest. I'd like a bride who really wants me. And though I'm resigned to this, I'd be lying if I said that I look forward to leaving The Desert Rose.''

"You're not much of a ladies' man."

Mac laughed. "Your conceited and totally wrong point being that I'm like a green stud who'd have to be shown what to do with a reluctant mare."

"Something like that."

Mac narrowed his eyes at Cade. "Are you offering to go to Balahar to smooth the waters between my bride and me? Sort of a romantic emissary?"

"I do a lot of traveling," Cade said. "You don't. In fact, you'll have to get your passport updated. You'll have to take a charm class. New duds and a suitable gift for your fiancée will be necessary. You don't have time for all of that."

"I hadn't thought of any of that stuff."

"You're too busy with the horses. I'm used to the business end of The Desert Rose. There wouldn't be much difference between conducting transactions for a prize horse or a bride."

"A princess."

"She should be *your* princess," Cade said softly. "Mac, I want you to have the woman of your dreams. That wouldn't matter so much for me, but it matters for you."

They stared at each other for a long moment. Cade could see his brother wavering. He knew his twin well. Mac would perform his duty, but his heart was sick over it. He couldn't bear to see Mac suffer.

"This is a mistake that could hurt you for a long time, Mac."

"But why? Why wouldn't it hurt you?"

Cade shrugged. "As Mother said, I don't take life as seriously as you do."

"So what would you do? Marry this woman and then leave her to her own devices?" Mac's voice was incredulous.

"I wouldn't get real worked up about it, that's for sure." Cade shrugged. "It's an arranged marriage. Once the princess learned her place, we'd probably get along fine. Anyway, all I'm suggesting is that we check her out first. Then you'll at least know what you're getting. Never buy merchandise you haven't handpicked, you know. You wouldn't buy a horse without checking its teeth, would you?"

Mac snorted. "I'd be glad to trade identities with you, because I don't think the princess is going to go for having her cheeks pinched open and her molars prodded."

"Let's pull straws." Cade grinned. "Short straw gets to visit the ugly princess."

Mac turned a bit pale. "Who said she was ugly?"

"Hey, if she was any great catch, her family would be raffling her off to some important nation, not trying to ship her off to us. If she's not ugly, then she's meaner than a bull that's short on mates. Trust me, this princess is a booby prize." He sighed heavily. "I'd be willing to bet she doesn't even ride a horse. Probably has some retainer ride her horse for her.''

"That's it! Get out the straws!''

Cade grinned at Mac's desperate tone. He snatched up two pieces of hay that lay nearby, chewing one short. Holding them up for Mac's inspection, he palmed them. "Draw.''

Mac swallowed. Reluctantly he took the straw Cade had placed nearest him, as Cade had known Mac would. Mac never veered from his course. Even when they were kids, he'd always taken the straw closest to him. "Lucky you,'' Cade said, as Mac's face lit up. Cade put his straw in his back pocket. "You stay here and mind the heart of The Desert Rose. I'll go check out the princess's heart and let you know the lay of the land. I needed to be over in Saudi Arabia to meet with some potential clients anyway. This'll just be a minor detour.''

"I sure would appreciate it,'' Mac said gratefully.

Cade smiled.

"How are you going to pull this off, Cade?''

"We'll simply tell Mother you're going to take some time to think over the situation. She doesn't need to know I'm doing a little covert babe-watching. Since basically it would take our mother or a fingerprint to give away the fact that I'm not you, I don't see it as a problem. It's not like they're going to lay down the red carpet for Prince Makin until a formal decision is reached, bro. From what I gather from Mother, this whole marriage thing has to be pretty hush-hush so that old King Azzam doesn't find out and start up with his evil bag of tricks again.''

Mac shook his head. "I gotta be honest, I'm not much for political intrigue."

"I know. It's definitely a drawback to the good life." Cade smirked.

"It's hell having to ask your brother to possibly be assassinated in your place."

The smirk was instantly replaced by a frown. "Who the hell said anything about me being assassinated for you? I'll be in and out of the country so fast Azzam will never even know I was there." He smiled reassuringly at his brother. "Don't worry so much. I can pull this off without a hitch."

THE TRUTH WAS, of course, that Cade had made certain he had the short straw. He didn't want his brother to go to Balahar. Mac wasn't cut out for marriage to a woman he didn't know or love, especially a princess who could very likely turn out to be hard to handle.

Cade, on the other hand, had loved women with all the enthusiasm of a handsome, confident male who knew how to please a lady, and make her feel like a princess when the morning hours dawned and it was time to say goodbye. A difficult woman was more his forte than Mac's.

More than anything, it would hurt him to see his twin suffer. If Mac was happy, then Cade would be happy.

This was the wrong time for a woman to be foisted on Mac. Cade was a little annoyed that his mother didn't recognize this fact. Mac had been engaged some time ago and nearly made it down the aisle when he discovered his fiancée was pregnant by another man. Talk about heartbreak. Cade sighed.

And then at their cousin Jessica's graduation from the University of Texas last December, Mac had slipped away for the evening. Seeing Mac the next morning, Cade tried to pry out of his brother where he'd been the night before. Mac was elusive, and Cade suspected his brother had met a mystery woman. But if he had, he refused to be teased into an admission.

That was Mac, though, Cade thought. If it had been Cade, he would have written the whole matter off as a windfall adventure. He might have thought about the woman again, but not often.

No, going to Balahar to make certain his already-wounded brother wasn't getting saddled with a rack pony as opposed to the wonderful woman his brother deserved was a job Cade would gladly undertake.

Royalty be damned.

"I WILL NOT MARRY HIM," Princess Serena insisted. "There are plenty of princes from whom I can make my own choice.''

King Zak sighed at his adopted child's insistence. Adopted maybe, but no less a daughter of his heart. ''I want you to be happy. I need also to make certain that peace is achieved between our country and that of Sorajhee. I am not asking you to be a brood mare, a sacrificial lamb. This marriage with an old family of royal standing and popularity among our people would pacify the peoples of Sorajhee and Balahar. Could you not just meet Prince Makin?''

''I will meet him,'' Serena said with a toss of her head. Rich, light emerald eyes flashed with determination, and her chestnut tresses shone with fire. ''I will meet him, and I will be a dutiful daughter to the father who has been so good to me. But I promise you one thing. I will not love him, this royal pretender to our throne. He will be haughty and overbearing, as all Americans are. He can never fit into my world. Just because he breeds Arabians does not mean he will breed with this one.''

''Rena!'' King Zak murmured with some surprise. ''You are more American than you think. Your father's bloodline left his mark on you in more ways than one.''

''I have grown up in Balahar. I could never be American. The idea of marrying a cowboy makes me—'' She faltered at the distressed look on her adopted father's face. ''I will do it,'' she murmured.

Slowly she moved forward to kiss the king on the cheek. "Please pardon my unforgivable loss of composure. I know you are doing the best thing."

"You do understand?" King Zak asked with relief.

"I do. If I were ruler and had the choices set out before me that you do, I would choose no differently. I, too, love Balahar and its people."

"Ah, Rena," the king sighed, placing her soft hand against his face. "You have been the daughter to me that Queen Nadirah and I prayed for and were never granted. Thank you, my daughter. I promise you this will all work out for the best."

Serena closed her eyes as she stroked her father's cheek. If she was lucky, the cowboy prince wouldn't be brash and mean, a J.R. Ewing looking to take over the Middle East with this marriage. There was much to gain for her would-be suitor, and much for her to lose. Her freedom. Her pride. Her dream of falling in love with a prince of her own. She might not have been Al Farid by birth, but she had grown to love the country. A prince of the Middle East had been her most fervent hope.

Prince Makin would come to meet with her. She would accept his suit. They would agree to a royal match that would benefit everyone and the countries involved, and most especially the father she loved more than anything

But she would never, ever love Prince Makin. That was something no one could ask of her.

Her heart was her most closely guarded treasure, and it would never belong to a pretender.

Chapter Two

"I hear rumors that the Princess Serena may be marrying," Queen Layla whispered into her husband's ear.

"Whom would she marry? There are few princes available who would suit Al Farid's daughter." Azzam chuckled and got up from the bed. "Why not a marriage for his son, Sharif?"

"Sharif is young and hotheaded, while Serena, though young, is more amenable to her father's wishes. Or perhaps Zakariyya Al Farid is hoping that this more minor marriage of his daughter will build the people's faith in his rule and give him more time to make a truly advantageous match for Crown Prince Sharif, one that befits a future king— should Zakariyya decide to give the ruling family throne to a foundling child rather than unite with you."

The last words came out on a near snarl that Layla managed to temper at the last second. She rose up on her side, trying to recapture her husband's full attention with the alluring pose. "Possibly you should have a word with the king, in order to assist him with the proper choice for his princess. I am certain he would appreciate your counsel."

Azzam glanced back to Layla, his attention captured by her words and not her pose. "Are you suggesting that the adopted daughter of the king could present a threat to my rule of my own Sorajhee throne? Power doesn't come through princesses."

Layla uncomfortably thought about Rose Coleman and the four boys she'd delivered. Why couldn't Layla have been so blessed by Allah? Moreover, why couldn't Layla have won Ibrahim in the first place, rather than Rose winning his heart? All the years of secrecy, pain and betrayal had begun in the moment the American Rose had stolen Ibrahim's heart. If he had chosen Layla, she would have had the sons, the heirs to the Sorajhee throne.

All she'd gained in the years since she'd had Ibrahim assassinated and Rose incarcerated in the asylum was fading looks and declining power in the region. Even if she had the Balahar ruler assassinated, there was a crown prince. And Serena, and a possible new marriage to an El Jeved prince, according to her palace spy. There were many problems that stood in her way.

Particularly if the Coleman-El Jeved princes ever came to press their right to the throne.

She glanced at her husband as a maidservant assisted him with his robes. He wasn't the young, vibrant male she'd married with great hopes. Sometimes she thought he was content to allow King Zakariyya Al Farid to rule both Balahar *and* Sorajhee. How could he be so complacent! Being number two had never sat well with Layla.

And now the new information of a rumored marriage for Serena Al Farid. The girl was of age. A marriage was not what bothered Layla. King Zak had not bothered to discuss the union with Azzam, a fact of importance that seemed to escape her husband. The secrecy and planning of the marriage meant that evermore the Balahar throne slipped further from Azzam, leaving him with only the smaller country of Sorajhee.

Layla sighed. Once again she would have to assist her husband. Behind the scenes, as always, a fact which galled her. Surely she had not erred by stealing Rose Coleman's youngest son and secretly giving him to King Zak and the now-deceased Queen Nadirah—as a seeming gesture of caring—to raise? This irony unsettled her. Until she realized that King Zak could be planning to marry off his daughter without consulting Azzam, she had not thought her husband's position as supreme ruler was in jeopardy. But with the queen dead and Zak unwilling to seek solace amongst his harem, possibly he was feeling all his powers waning from him and was setting out to shape the new destiny of the country—without consulting the rightful king.

Azzam should be king of both countries, and she should be queen, set far above the petty scurrying she was forever forced to do to maintain their importance in the Balahar-Sorajhee union.

One day, Layla vowed, *she* would be queen, with subjects who adored only her.

IF THERE WAS ONE THING that occupied Mac's mind more than what Cade was attempting on his behalf, it was the unfinished business he'd left behind the night of his cousin Jessica's graduation. What had he been thinking by spending a night with one of his cousin's friends?

But the lady he'd met had been so pretty. She was gentle and quiet, with brown hair like a baby deer and eyes so blue he felt he could see Texas heaven in them. Cade had been right: Mac did take life seriously. He didn't sleep around, and he didn't treat women like interchangeable dates.

Something had happened to him when he'd met the woman the night Jessica graduated. Sizzle hotter than fire and electricity more powerful than a horse's kick had jump-started him into believing that maybe there was a woman out there for him, a sweet woman who was as different from his ex-fiancée as he could possibly find.

And then she'd been gone. Before he'd had a chance to know everything about her that he desperately wanted to know, the girl he'd known for only a stolen interlude of lovemaking had vanished with the dawn.

He should be happy. No promises, no strings.

But a spark had touched his heart when he least expected it, and when his mother had mentioned him marrying a princess, he'd felt his heart open a none-too-healed wound.

With this new worry that his mother was intent upon securing a royal match for him—and knowing that the time Cade was buying for him was all too short—Mac needed to do something he had stead-fastly avoided doing.

He had to try to get Jessica to reveal the name of her friend without her figuring out what he was up to. This would be no easy accomplishment. Jessica was smart and quick and merciless with teasing where her cousins were concerned, a payback for all the years they'd lovingly teased her about the two-colored eyes she possessed. If she thought a woman was on his mind, Jessica would ferret out who, what, when and where.

That could be a disaster. Knowing Jessica, she'd probably conjure up the dream girl for him. Which didn't seem quite fair, since he wasn't positive the girl would want to see him. They had, after all, ren-dered a tacit agreement between them to let the night of pleasure be enough for both of them.

He was not a man to go back on his word, spoken or unspoken.

But he had no choice. Jessica was the only one who held the information he needed.

Going to the stables, he found her grooming the stallion Jabbar. Older, but still a handsome Arabian, Jabbar tolerated very few people near him. Jessica and Jabbar seemed to have an understanding about how much grooming a male could tolerate. Jabbar certainly didn't mind her light touch.

Of course, Jabbar didn't have to put up with anything but gentle coaxing and praise from Jessica. Mac, on the other hand, was of no mind to be on the teasing side of her tongue.

"Jess," he said quietly, so that he wouldn't startle her or the stallion.

"Hey, Mac." She sent a smile his way but continued single-mindedly with her task.

Maybe this was the best time to quiz her, when her attention was fully engaged elsewhere, Mac decided on a hopeful note. "I was looking at some pictures from your graduation today."

She smiled but didn't look up. "Were you?"

"Yeah." He scratched at his chin. "I was surprised you graduated so high in your class."

A snort greeted his words. "I was surprised that you graduated at all."

He smiled. This light banter covered his deeper mission. "I was somewhat amazed you had so many friends. Obviously they got to see a side of you we never do."

"Shut up, cousin. I reserve my best side for you."

"Ahem." Nonchalantly he peered into another stall before glancing at Jess's stoic face. "Wondered if you were planning on having any of your friends out to the ranch. If you're missing your buddies, you know you're welcome."

She shook her head. "I'm going on a girl's-only trip with a bunch of them soon. One of them is getting married, so we're going to have a bachelorette vacation. If everybody's going to start getting married, this may be the last time we can all get together like this."

His heart fell into his boots. "Really? Who's going down the aisle?"

A curious glance came his way. "Why are you asking?"

He shrugged.

She raised a brow. "I don't think you'd know her."

"I might." *I might know her better than you think.*

Turning back to inspect Jabbar's coat, she said, "Susie Anderson."

No. He had not made love with a Susie, he'd be willing to bet. His heart lifted. "Your friends all seemed real nice. The ones I got to meet at graduation anyway."

She nodded. "Thanks."

This was definitely a dead end. He couldn't come right out and ask her about some girl and give her a description without her figuring out why he was asking.

"Aunt Rose mentioned that you're probably going to be taking a little trip of your own soon," Jessica said, glancing at him with a saucy smile. "A honeymoon maybe."

He stared at her, his eyes wide with shock at hearing her speak what he didn't want to think about. There was no way he could ask Jess about one of her girlfriends when he was as good as promised to another woman.

"Maybe," was all he said as he fled the stable.

ROSE DIDN'T BELIEVE for one minute that her sons intended to fall in willingly with an arranged marriage. Prince Makin had been shocked and might have gone along with it, but yesterday Prince Kadar had possessed a mischievous glint in his eyes that spelled a rocky road ahead for the plan. She smiled to herself. Kadar would require a much defter hand when it came time to plan his engagement. If only he knew how much an Arabian prince he truly was! His wife would be hard-pressed to keep him out of the harem.

Of course, Ibrahim had been much like Kadar in his appreciation of women—until he'd met her. Perhaps it was simply finding the one woman of Kadar's heart for him to be captured completely.

It had not escaped her notice that Makin was more reticent than ever when it came to dating, even stating once that he would never marry. That's why she'd thought that he was best suited for an arranged match with Serena Al Farid—notwithstanding the fact that he was the son second in line in the ascension.

How much she would like her sons to regain their rightful place! Pulling this marriage off before Azzam discovered it would be fortunate beyond words. Her princes deserved their father's heritage.

She hadn't counted on Kadar's very definite opposition to his twin's engagement. Perhaps in time he would come to see that Makin, with his avowed dislike of dating, could best benefit by this arrangement. It would not require his heart to be involved, which might suit Makin just fine.

Perhaps she needed to explain her thoughts to Kadar. Having him understand that she hadn't coldly arranged this match out of a desire for power could be the key. She went in search of him in his quarters.

Kadar's room was empty. Rose turned, meeting Ella in the hallway.

"Have you seen Cade?" Rose asked the housekeeper.

Ella gave her a strange look. "He left for Saudi Arabia this afternoon, remember?"

How could she have forgotten! This marriage weighed so heavily on her mind. "I had forgotten. Thank you for reminding me."

It didn't matter. She could talk to him when he returned from his business trip. A few days wouldn't make any difference, and would give her time to work on Makin.

"Ella," Rose said suddenly, turning to call after her. "Do you happen to know if Mac is in the house?"

"He went to look at some foals up in the Panhandle. Didn't he tell you? He said he was going to." Now Ella's expression was perplexed.

Rose shook her head before she could give away her own surprise. It wasn't like Makin to disappear like that! Perhaps her suggestion of an arranged marriage had rattled him more than he wanted to admit.

Then again, a few days to himself to digest the startling suggestion she'd put forth might be the best thing.

For just a moment, Rose wondered if Kadar was up to something. It was strange that both men were gone at once.

Then she shrugged it off. Kadar and Makin were grown men. They wouldn't do anything rash.

CADE WAS ASTONISHED when his plane was met by a respectful retinue of men dressed in long robes and head ornamentation. Though he was wearing jeans and boots, he went through the traditional Arabian greetings.

"Welcome, Prince Makin," one serious-looking official said to him.

Cade started. "I—" He swallowed. This was the time to come clean, to say that he was not the prince they thought. "I am happy to be here," he said. All he'd done was place a call to the king's adviser to let him know he'd dash by for a quick meeting with the ruler before he went on his travels. He hadn't expected the royal treatment!

"The king awaits your arrival," a taller man said, pointing Cade toward a black Mercedes limo.

Cade got in. *I'm doing this for my brother. I can handle lunch with the king. It's not an afternoon of business golf or anything. It's lunch, a little schmoozing, hopefully a sneak peek at the princess, and I'm outta here.*

His stomach tightened as the five stern-looking officials fitted themselves into the limo around him. It was clear that this was a mission of utmost dignity for them. The bulletproof windows were meaningful evidence that everything about this mission was important. His brother would not have enjoyed this grave treatment at all.

Any princess that lives with this bunch of stiffs guarding her is probably going to be a pain in the rump, he told himself.

I'm doing the right thing for Mac.

PRINCESS SERENA Wilson-Al Farid allowed her maidservants to dress her in silence. To her surprise, Serena had learned that her intended groom was already on the way from the airport to meet her. Apparently he was more eager than she for the match. In one way, it was a compliment to her.

In another way, it had to mean that Prince Makin was very interested in solidifying his position within the royal family and possibly securing a future throne for himself. This was the most likely scenario, and Serena had to admit she didn't much like the sensation that she was merely a marital chip to one man's ambition.

And yet that was the reality of her situation.

"You are beautiful, Princess," she was duly informed.

It wouldn't matter if she were as ugly as intrigue, but she nodded in thanks for the compliment.

The ladies bowed their heads to her respectfully as they filed from the room. Serena glanced down at the shimmering cloth that had been skillfully draped to cover her and yet reveal her feminine charms and beauty. Amethyst with gold adornment highlighted her hair and the depth of her eyes.

It was all rather wasted on an American cowboy.

She could only pray that Prince Makin was kind, that he was at least handsome enough that she could stand to look at him in the light of day, and that he wasn't overly impressed with himself. Americans tended to think highly of themselves. Men in general were that way.

If he was a man who thought he was going to ride in and carry her off on his Arabian stallion, Serena thought she would have to really bite down hard to keep her dismay in check.

She would know in less than thirty minutes.

In the hallway outside, the sound of maids scurrying with excitement caught her attention. That meant the arrival of the prince.

Serena closed her eyes to compose herself and waited for her maids to fetch her.

The door flew open.

"He's here! The prince has arrived!" her ladies announced with glee.

Serena stared at them. "And the palace gossip says he is…?" she prompted.

They looked back at her uneasily.

"Out with it," she told them. "Prepare me for the worst."

"Tall," was the first response.

"Loud," was the second.

"Not dressed appropriately," was the third. "Not like a prince."

Serena's eyebrows rose.

"Jeans, a cowboy hat and boots, my lady," her most trusted handmaiden explained.

Serena drew herself up, unwilling to allow palace gossip to titter over the depth of her dismay. Nor would she embarrass her bridegroom with her reluctance.

"Take me to him," she said.

Chapter Three

The minute he stepped into the palace, Cade knew he'd underestimated the warmth of welcome extended to Prince Makin. King Zak's idea of hush-hush apparently didn't extend to a close gathering of advisers. A large room Cade would have described as a ballroom was filled with people wearing lavish ceremonial dress and jewels. It was a greeting meant to please and impress a future ruler.

King Zak apparently felt that to do any less would be to insult Prince Makin.

"Balahar and its king welcome Prince Makin," a courtier announced.

Cade was led forward. He saw beautiful woman after beautiful woman, all with their eyes downcast as he passed them. If he were in a different position, he would have been strongly inclined to take advantage of the wealth of loveliness temptingly displayed before him.

The king of Balahar sat on a throne at the end of

the room, his face lit with a proud smile. Cade was ushered to within two feet of the regal king. He bowed deeply, only rising when the king touched his shoulder.

And then Cade saw the princess. She was brought forward from somewhere behind the throne, and took her place to the side of the king. She was arrayed in stunning purple and gold, and more strands of gold laced through magnificently burnished hair that reached her waist. Cade could see her eyes because she didn't keep them lowered as he knew custom dictated. Nor did she curtsy as her maidservants were frantically indicating she should. She merely looked at him evenly with fabulous emerald eyes that assessed him as he did her.

She wasn't tall, but she wasn't petite, either.

In fact, she was just the perfect height for him. She watched him, and he watched her, and the whole court waited, enveloped in a hush.

He'd never seen a woman like her. The words that blew into his mind weren't royal in the least: *What a babe! She's a goddess. Mac's gonna have a fit when he sees how lucky he is!*

The princess never blinked as he stared, her perusal so thorough and honest that he had to smile. He'd been checked out by females before, but this lady left coyness to her Arabian sisters. He could tell his jeans and boots didn't necessarily agree with her but that something about him caught her interest in spite of herself.

So she was as reluctant as Mac was. *And not about to get caught buying a stallion without checking out its molars, either.*

Cade couldn't help himself. She was an absolute doll. He grinned hugely at her.

The court erupted with excited whispers and muted applause.

"Welcome to the family, Prince Makin," King Zak said. "Your acceptance of my daughter, Serena, brings great joy to my heart."

SERENA'S HEART JUMPED in her chest when her father spoke the words from which there was no going back. *It's done,* she thought wildly as the chattering voices swirled around her. King Zak embraced his new son-in-law, and then the prince bowed before her, taking her hand in his as he kissed her fingers.

Shock ran through her. The cowboy prince was not following custom, and it caught her off guard. Strange feelings of excitement ran through her at the touch of his lips brushing her skin. Amazement rippled over her as she hesitated, unsure as to what she should do next. What did he expect from her?

"Smile for me, Princess," he said softly, for her ears alone.

His husky command threw her into confusion.

That voice sought her compliance, made her want to do whatever he wanted of her.

This was not the way she wanted to feel about a husband she wished to feel nothing for.

Even for a princess who knew her duty, the magnetic appeal seeking to steal her senses was overwhelming. Before Serena could force herself to obey her prince, her cowardly legs managed a brief curtsy before she escaped to the shelter of her room.

I cannot do this! I cannot marry a man who looks at me as if he could devour me with a single kiss!

WITHIN MOMENTS, her maidservants came for her. There was no escaping her fate now that Prince Makin had nodded his acceptance of their arranged marriage. Her hair was swiftly combed to hang free to her waist, no longer adorned with the gold ribbons. Perfume meant to tantalize her bridegroom was lavishly dabbed at her temples and between her breasts.

She was taken to a small antechamber where the king and Prince Sharif—King Zak's other adopted child—and her own prince awaited her. The look on Prince Makin's face was somehow priceless. He'd been pried from his jeans and robed in raiment befitting an Arabian prince for his marriage. Because of the need for swiftness and utmost secrecy, the only other people in the room were the king's trusted adviser, her favorite maidservant, and the official who would bless their union. Momentarily she wondered if Prince Makin was taken aback by the lack of pomp surrounding their marriage, but that was impossible. It was his mother, Rose Coleman-El Jeved, who had emphasized the need for such.

The ceremony was over in a matter of moments, which flew by all too quickly. Numbly Serena realized that not only was she now irrevocably married to the American pretender, he fully intended to claim a kiss from her. Heart rate accelerating, she closed her eyes and prayed the kiss would be mercifully swift.

FOR A MAN USED TO THINKING on his feet, Cade would later admit to himself and everyone else that he'd been caught totally off guard. First off, he hadn't realized that a simple smile meant he was accepting the princess as his. Second, he would have to confess that his command of Arabian hadn't prepared him for the swift rush as he was led to a private chamber where his clothes were swiftly replaced with more appropriate ones. Realizing he was in over his head, Cade opted to keep his mouth shut.

To admit now that he was not Prince Makin would bring such embarrassment upon the family name it couldn't even be considered. And he could only envision the humiliation on his mother's face if he were found out. Prince Sharif stared at him with an enigmatic smile on his face, one dark eyebrow raised, his lips curled as if he owned the world. And as if he could read Cade's discomfort with the trap he'd gotten himself jammed in.

Cade's gaze shifted to the golden trap named Serena. He was stuck with this lovely woman. From the frantic, frightened look on her face, he figured they were both roped into a corral neither of them wanted to share.

Maybe it was the oh-no-he's-going-to-eat-me look on Serena's face that drove him to do what he sensed she didn't want him to do. But he was a prince, and that meant he could kiss his bride if he wanted to, and somehow he'd gotten himself tangled up in this rope, and by jimmy, she could just share his misery.

Cade put his lips against the startled princess's. Like beating butterfly wings spreading apart, her mouth opened under his.

All Cade could think of when he felt her compliant surrender was that after all the years his mother had dragged him to church, he finally understood what King Solomon had been so excited about when he'd written his famous Song of Solomon.

As impossible as it seemed, as wrong as it should have been to touch the princess intended for his brother, kissing Serena Al Farid made Cade feel like a powerful and wealthy-beyond-measure king.

Serena Wilson-Al Farid was a treasure.

Chapter Four

"My spies tell me that the marriage is done," Layla informed Azzam, "and the fact that we were not invited is insulting."

"None were invited," Azzam consoled her. "Put it from your mind."

"I can't." Layla was festering inside. Azzam's lack of concern for the situation distressed her to the point of pressing him. "Azzam, you trust Zak too much!"

Azzam shrugged. "I truly don't have the thirst for intrigue that I once did."

"I do," she replied, her voice bitter. "The throne of Sorajhee is the only prize left to me in my old age and I would see the jewel polished more brightly."

"You speak like a foolish old woman."

Pride mixed with impatience stirred up a vicious cocktail inside Layla. "You would not speak so if you knew everything I have done to protect what is rightfully yours! How can you even speak of allowing Zakariyya to take it from you?''

Azzam's eyes narrowed on her. "I doubt the wisdom in not exacting a punishment for your previous schemes. What have you done for me, besides be a choking bone in my throat with your constant demands for more power? More of everything? You wear me out, woman. No wonder I spend more time than ever in the comparative peace of my harem.''

Layla cloaked herself inside her robe, drawing the cloth tight against her body, a shield against his scorn. The beginning of hatred for her husband ate into her soul. What a blow to her pride that, after all the years she'd worked to make certain no Coleman-El Jeveds made a claim to the throne, one had apparently appeared like a bad dream from the past to do just that. She should have done more than convince Azzam to put Rose into a sanitarium and steal Rose's one son away from her. She should have demanded to see the bodies of the three other Coleman-El Jeved princes when they were rumored to have died. But she'd been so certain that having Rose shut away would end any future threat to Azzam ascending to the throne. "I will take my leave of you now," she said frostily as she bowed to Azzam. "If you will grant me so.''

He shrugged, losing interest in his petulant wife. With that cool dismissal, Layla swept from the room. *Fool not to see the danger under your very nose, Azzam!*

But she did. And it was up to her to make certain that nothing stood in between her and the prize she coveted above all.

Balahar.

Fortunately, she had a few moves left to her. If the marriage was not consummated tonight, it would not be a legal and biding union. She had learned that the American was on his way to a neighboring country.

Between now and the time he departed, Serena's new husband would find it very difficult to consummate the royal marriage.

She smiled to herself, and thanked Allah for inhibiting potions and loyal spies.

SERENA AND CADE sat beside each other at a table draped with a lavish cloth and more food than they could eat. A robed servant stood behind them, anticipating their dining needs. Cade ignored the tea the servant moved closer to his plate. He didn't need tea, or food for that matter.

What he needed was to talk to Serena, and she hadn't uttered more than two words to him so far. Did she plan to ignore him?

"Guess you're not too crazy about being married to me," he stated mildly.

"I am positive I could say the same about you."

She gave him a frank look that plainly said she was being restrained.

"I have to say you're a relief," Cade began, thinking to compliment the princess. "I was afraid you'd be..."

"Ugly?" Serena supplied.

He grinned. "Maybe on the unattractive side."

"I am glad you do not find me so. I, on the other hand, thought you'd be a white and pasty American. I, too, find you a relief."

Cade straightened. "You had to have known my family history. My father was Arab."

"You are still darker than I expected." Her eyes followed a trail of bare skin at his neck, and then skipped the covering of the robe to examine his hands. "And not the spoiled good-for-nothing playboy I was expecting. You have the hands of a man who works hard."

"You watch too many American TV shows," Cade said with a smile. The servant had moved the tea glass yet closer to his plate, and Cade pushed it away. "What other misconception can I clear up for you?"

"I have to be honest with you, Prince Makin," Serena said, startling Cade with the subject of honesty and reminding him that he had a little truth he needed to share with her as well. "I dreamed of choosing a prince of my own, an Arabian of royal birth. I love it here in Balahar and would not wish to leave. I am far more Arab than I am American.''

"I'm far more American than I am Arab.'' He thought about that. There was no way Mac was going to live in Balahar: he wouldn't be happy here at all. Cade thought palace life would try his patience after more than a few days. ''I think you're going to end up living in America again, Princess.''

"I do not wish to leave my people.''

"You married me,'' he said bluntly. ''What did you expect?''

"Frankly, I expected you were marrying me to be in line for the throne.''

"Nope.'' He pushed the goblet away for a final time, looking up at the servant. ''Take the tea away. I do not want it.''

The servant jumped to remove the glass, his expression concerned. Cade couldn't explain it, but something about the servant bothered him unreasonably. Maybe he was just tense from this princess problem. He turned his attention back full force to Serena. ''I can tell you quite honestly that none of the Coleman males are interested in the Balahar throne.''

"Why do you say it that way?'' Delicate chestnut eyebrows lifted with surprise.

"Just letting you know, Princess, in case you thought you'd married the wrong brother. We're all the same on this subject.'' It was the truth. Even if he weren't masquerading as Mac, Cade would never be interested in this whole scenario.

Except maybe for the princess. He eyed her covertly over the food they both ignored. She was gorgeous and sexy, a hottie in gauzy fabric. But he couldn't see her with Mac.

Uh-oh. I don't even want to have this thought.

"Listen, princess—"

"Do you mind calling me by my name?" she asked. "Somehow, when you say *princess*, I'm pretty sure you're not expressing a term of respect. I feel you could just as easily interchange *babe, doll,* or *sweet cheeks* for *princess.* And I don't like it."

She glared at him.

Caught by surprise, he hesitated before grinning widely.

"It's your attitude," she told him. "And your tone. I prefer you address me as Serena when we are alone together."

"Anything else you want from me, Serena?"

"All I ask is that you always be honest with me. I didn't expect a love match, but I would appreciate honesty and respect."

"All right." He tossed the napkin onto the table, unable to eat the strongly spiced food. "I did expect a pampered princess who would be mainly an ornament."

"So sorry to disappoint you." Her eyes blazed at him.

He drummed the table, causing the servant to jump to anticipate Cade's needs. This put Cade into a worse mood, not the least because the tea he hadn't wanted was replaced with something else—which he wouldn't drink, either. "Can we ditch this guy? He's like a jumpy puppy."

The first hint of a smile he'd seen on Serena's face came and went quickly—but it had been there. "I don't mind."

He waved a hand to dismiss the servant, who backed reluctantly from the room. "So, I'll leave you here while I finish my business and then come back and get you sometime," Cade offered.

"You do not intend to…to—"

"I don't think so," he interrupted. "It would be better if we didn't."

"But the marriage won't be binding unless it's consummated."

"Do you want it to be binding?" He looked at her curiously.

"I—I'm not sure," she admitted. "I don't think we have much in common. Yet it would break my father's heart."

There was that. His mother would be none too pleased, either, especially when she discovered what he'd done.

"Don't you want to make love to me?" she asked suddenly.

His throat dried out. His entire body electrified at

her soft question. "I do, Princess," he said, without a trace of the mockery with which he'd referred to her before. "But you want honesty, and you deserve that from your husband. And I can't give that to you right now."

"What do you mean?"

He sighed. Then he leaned close to her ear, which brought the scent of her to him fully and made him somehow regret what he had to tell her. "I'm not Prince Makin," he said.

SERENA HELD BACK A SMILE, thinking this prince had a strange sense of humor. "Of course you are Prince Makin. My father would know if you were not."

"I have a twin, who is Prince Makin. I am Prince Kadar."

She raised an eyebrow. "If that is true, why are you lying to my father? To the people of Balahar?"

"I had no intention of marrying you when I came here," he said. She sensed the honesty behind his striking words. "Everything happened quickly. There didn't seem to be a good time to pull the reins in, actually. And once I realized that I'd agreed to marry you, I didn't want to insult King Zak by saying that I'd changed my mind."

"I see." Serena tried to hold back her rising dismay. "No, I don't see. So you didn't marry me for the throne of Balahar."

"No."

He shook his head, and a vague sense of feminine insult, no matter how irrational it should have been, rose inside her. "Where is Prince Makin, your brother, then? The man I was intended to marry?"

"At home, tending to The Desert Rose."

"You are his emissary. He sent you to spy on me."

"No. Well, maybe. I had business over in Saudi Arabia and said I'd pop by and visit you. This wasn't the way I intended for the visit to work out, obviously."

"You'd *pop* by and visit me. How American that sounds." She was starting to feel more than a trace of bitterness. "So you popped by and married me instead."

One dark brow rose as he stared at her. "You have every right to be angry. I fully expect that we can have this marriage annulled because it won't be consummated. Then you can marry my twin, who is your proper intended."

"Or?" Now her brow rose. "I assume there's an 'or' in this."

He shrugged. "You could come home with me. I'm not flying commercially, and my co-pilot is waiting at the airport, so we'd have plenty of secrecy."

"The purpose of coming with you would be?"

"Popping by and checking out Mac. Turnabout is fair play, I suppose."

She refused to smile at his suggestion, although his tone suggested irony. "Prince Kadar, I am not a plaything."

"I am not suggesting you are." He leaned close to where she sat, touching her hair with a reverent finger. "Quite the opposite. You are the most beautiful woman I've ever seen."

Both her brows rose in astonishment. "I find that difficult to believe from such a playboy."

"I am not a playboy!"

"A man who 'pops' by a foreign country to check out the goods is obviously a connoisseur. Or else your brother wouldn't have sent you," she stated with conviction. "Besides, your very personality tells me that you are too confident that no matter what situation you find yourself in, you always find a way to turn it to your advantage." She raised her chin. "I do not like that trait in you. You remind me of Prince Sharif."

"I wouldn't compare me to a spoiled prince."

"Oh?" She smiled without the sentiment behind it. "You know so much about him then, in the thirty minutes you've seen him?"

"He reminds me of someone I know." His voice was thoughtful. "And he doesn't like me, I can tell."

"How intuitive of my brother, then," she said

sarcastically. "To mistrust a man who is lying to him, marries his sister under false pretenses, and is no more a real prince than any commoner living outside these walls."

"I am from the family I say I am," Cade said sternly.

"It takes more than the accident of royal blood to make a prince," Serena retorted. "Do not disparage my brother in the future. And don't try to turn this particular situation to your advantage. I refuse to be manipulated for your purposes." She crossed her arms. "Why should I not go to my father this instant and tell him what you've done?"

"Because I think you know that I mean you no harm. And I understand you being a little insulted that I don't want to stay married to you, but you have to understand that my brother is—"

"I think I'll keep you," Serena said suddenly. "The punishment for your rash behavior should be to deal with your actions."

"Hey, Princess, I'm not a child or one of your servants to command—"

"No, but you have wronged me. Do not play the injured party when it is me, Prince Kadar." Serena could tell he didn't like the tables being turned on him one bit, and that feeling of power provoked her into words. "You find me beautiful. I find you somewhat handsome."

"Somewhat handsome!"

"Somewhat. Passably," Serena said, glossing over the feminine fib. "I'm assuming I'd find your twin just as attractive, but he let you steal me away from him and I can't admire that in a man."

"Wait! I didn't mean to steal you."

"I am not in a mind to have my marriage annulled," she cut in. "Already there are people who wish to see my father undermined, and such hesitation would definitely factor in weakness."

"I don't follow your thinking, Princess."

"Of course you do not. You have not lived among palace spies and royal intrigue all your life. Quite simply, within moments of this problem getting out, those who wish harm to my father would know. And they would use the time needed to annul this marriage to their advantage. In other words, I can't risk the danger to my father by playing games. You are married to me, and you will stay so."

"That sounds dangerously like a command, Princess."

She heard the steel in his voice and saw the glint in his eyes. This was a man who did not like to be pushed around. He had strength in him.

He would be good for Balahar and Sorajhee.

Allah provided in strange ways, but those ways should not be questioned by a princess who wanted more than anything the best for her people.

"It is not a command, my prince," she said, her soft voice masking her determination. "It is merely a favor I am asking in return for a situation you brought on me not of my making. I know you to be a man who will take responsibility for your actions, and who would not wish to bring embarrassment upon me or my father."

He considered her suddenly gentle point in silence. Serena could tell he was thinking over her words, although he wasn't terribly happy.

"You will have to explain to your brother, of course, that the two of you made a plan between you that did not work out the way you'd hoped." She gave a delicate shrug. "But if he sent you in his place I think he will not mind too much that I will be yours instead of his."

That was truth. Kadar never blinked, confirming her suspicions that Prince Makin had not been amenable to the match. She did not want a husband who did not want her. At university in America, she had learned many quaint expressions, and one of them was that the devil one knew was better than a devil one didn't.

And this devil wasn't totally hellish. He would be strong for Balahar, and she found him appealing as a man. For an extra moment she examined her motives, to make certain it was not her feminine heartstrings that spoke to her reluctance to give up this man.

The servant entered the room, moving forward with more food and yet a different drink for Prince

Kadar, and Serena was decided. "Leave us," she told the servant.

The servant obeyed readily.

"Don't drink that," Serena told Kadar.

"Why not?"

She had expected him to question her. "It is drugged."

His gaze went to the goblet again before returning to her. "Okay, first, were you going to let me drink the tea he'd given me before, and second, why are you harboring a palace spy?"

"You made no move to drink the tea, so you were safe. My father is trying to make his honored guest feel at home. He is honoring you, and you would drink and eat in recognition of your host's efforts. The spy is counting on your manners for the best chance at drugging you."

"Oh. I apologize for not falling in with the plan."

She shot him a dry glance. "I am harboring, as you put it, a palace spy because it is better to keep the spy that I know. If I get rid of him, Queen Layla will merely find another weak link in the palace to do her dirty work. And I wouldn't know who that one was for a while, which could be dangerous."

"The devil you know is better than the devil you don't." He grinned at her.

"Precisely my thought," she said mildly. "I am glad that we think so much alike. It bodes well for our marriage."

He shifted, suddenly on unfamiliar ground. "Why would anyone want to poison me, beyond the expected threat to the throne?"

She laughed softly at how tense his muscles had gone under his dark skin. Clearly this man did not like to be caught out of his element. "I suspect it is a drug to keep you from making love to me."

Straightening, he pulled slightly farther away from her. "I'm not going to make love to you."

"You're not?" Her voice held laughter. "Will you never want me, Prince Kadar?"

"I...I—" He stared at her, uncertain as to how to answer. "Are they going to try to drug me every day so I can't make love to you?"

"I suspect they know you are leaving Balahar soon. The servant will have immediately let them know any plans you might have mentioned to my father. In the future, you must remember that every wall hides a listening ear and absolutely no one is to be trusted."

"Hell of a way to exist," he grumbled.

"You seem to be able to think on your feet. You can survive once you learn some basic skills of royal life." She smiled at him encouragingly. "To get back to the dilemma we are facing, if you can't perform your princely duty before you leave," Serena said with a smile, "the marriage has a chance of being undone. It can be annulled. Queen Layla would have a chance to think of a hundred reasons why this marriage should not be. Maybe a thousand reasons, given the insult she will be feeling for not being invited to the wedding. As I said, it is not in Balahar's best interests for anything to undo our marriage. Thus, we must make love.''

She saw him take a deep breath, saw his eyes slide over her in a swift, assessing sweep. From the darkening of his pupils, there apparently was nothing he found repulsive about the task ahead of him.

''You think faster on your feet than I do. You'll have to give me a minute to think this through. I don't know that I can make love to a woman intended for my brother. My mind still thinks of you that way.''

She leaned close to him, near enough to tease him with her perfume and her femininity. ''Prince Kadar, your brother did not want me.''

''He didn't have a chance to find out.''

''The race goes to the swiftest,'' she said, placing her fingers lightly over his hand. ''In this case, the crown, with all its benefits and drawbacks, goes to the fastest warrior. That would be you, Prince Kadar.''

''Only because Mac—''

''You are my choice,'' she told him sincerely. ''His arranged marriage is now yours.''

She admired his consideration for his brother, Serena decided. He put other people's needs and wishes in front of his own. That was a quality a strong ruler needed. This was the right prince for Balahar.

"Prince Kadar, I promise you will not find me a clinging wife. I am an independent woman. You will not need to keep me entertained, nor treat me like the pampered lapdog you seem to have expected. I am a woman who wishes to put the country she loves first." She took a deep breath, knowing that Kadar's answer meant everything to her. "So, my husband, do you find me desirable enough to make love to me?"

Chapter Five

Cade's throat dried out as he stared at Serena. Was she kidding? Making love to her would be a dream come true; he could feel desire heating through him just by being this close to her.

He'd made love to enough women to know that loving Serena would be soul-claiming pleasure. He also knew that holding her and being one with her would be like nothing he'd known before.

It wasn't simply because she was his wife. Nor was it because she offered herself to him so sweetly and yet so forthrightly.

Serena was like no other woman he'd ever met— and it had nothing to do with her lineage. This woman would have stirred him if he'd met her in the meanest hut in the world.

She fascinated him.

"I would honestly enjoy making love to you," he said, his voice hoarse in a choked whisper he couldn't quite control. "Make no mistake about that."

Her eyes drew him in as she waited for him to speak. What could he say? There was no "but," no qualifier on the truth. He wanted to pull that flowing gauzy stuff off her slowly. Discovering her mysteries was as tantalizing as the thought of swirling through the veils of *Arabian Nights,* enjoying her one layer at a time.

He hadn't come to Balahar for a wife. Yet she was his wife. He was her husband.

He could search the entire earth and never find another woman like her.

But he could lose her.

"Call the spy back in here," he said suddenly.

She looked at him for a moment. He picked up the goblet and poured the liquid inside it into a nearby planter. Then he took her goblet and put the contents inside his.

"Shadi," she called loudly, her gaze on Kadar.

The servant entered a moment later.

"We are finished," she told him.

"Not quite, my princess," Cade said with a flourish. He lifted the goblet in a toast so that the servant could see—and then he drained it. "As delicious as your lips," he said airily.

Serena rolled her eyes, but since the servant stood obsequiously behind her chair, he could not see. Cade grinned to himself before yawning hugely. "I think I'll return to my room to shower," he said. "I will come to your room later."

Serena stood. "As you wish, my prince. Shadi will show you to your rooms."

"Great. I'm worn-out as an old hound dog," he said in his most exaggerated Texas accent.

The servant's expression was triumphant. Cade yawned again. The servant bowed, leading the way for him. "Bye, Princess," Cade said in an annoying voice. "Wait up for me."

Serena whirled on her low-heeled feet and fled the room. Cade smirked. "I'm following the yellow brick road, Shadi, unless you've got a magic carpet for me."

Shadi hurried down the hall into a long corridor. Cade strolled behind him leisurely. "Sure am tired after all the excitement, Shadi."

The servant barely glanced over his shoulder at Cade. Finally Shadi passed through an arch into a large room hung with heavy drapes and filled with furnishings fit for a prince. Cade threw himself down onto the bed, his body limp.

Silence told him Shadi was observing his position, making certain he was asleep. Cade didn't move a muscle.

After a moment, he heard the whispery sound of the servant disappearing from the room. Waiting another few minutes for good measure, Cade finally lifted himself off the bed.

"Prince Kadar," a voice said outside the open window of his room.

"Serena." He levered himself out of the window to stand beside her.

"You fake the effects of sleeping potion badly. Fortunately, Shadi seemed to buy your act."

He grinned at her. "I'd do anything to impress you, Princess."

"What was the need of pretending to drink the potion?"

"You said it was better to know who the spy was. He believes he has executed his task, and will rush back to let his commander know what a good soldier he is. In the meantime, you and I will head to my private jet and take off for Texas. It won't be the honeymoon you might have wanted, but under the circumstances, I think it's for the best. Let's get going before we're discovered."

She balked for an instant. "I must say goodbye to Father, and Prince Sharif."

"We can't risk it. The spy will know soon enough that the potion didn't work to his satisfaction."

"You are, of course, correct," Serena whispered unhappily. "If you are certain—"

"I believe it's the only way, Princess. With you faraway and safe at The Desert Rose, you are out of reach of spies and potions. We'll have time to get to know each other."

"You are not wishing to make love to me so fast?"

"I want to make love to you. But marriage is based on more than sex. And I don't like jumping around like a puppet because Princess Lana's pulling my strings."

"Queen Layla."

"Whatever." He shrugged. "The who doesn't matter. The what does, and the 'what' happens to be this marriage. I'll do what I want on my terms."

"You are not like other men," Serena said quietly. "And so I trust you. I will go with you, because I can tell you are doing what you believe to be right. Such a man makes the right decisions for many people."

They stared at each other for a long moment.

"Let's go," she said, putting on a black silk scarf that concealed all but her eyes. Her black *Jilba* disguised the rest of her. "I'm anxious to see this Texas that makes such strong men."

IF ROSE COLEMAN WAS SURPRISED that the wrong son came home with Princess Serena, she was too experienced at hiding her emotions to show it. She came forward to greet the princess with a hug. "Welcome to Texas, and to The Desert Rose, Princess Serena."

"Thank you." Serena smiled shyly at her new mother-in-law. "Texas seems as hot as Balahar."

Rose smiled. "The late summer months will be far closer to what you are used to. We will make you comfortable at The Desert Rose, though it isn't quite the palace."

"I have a feeling I will like this as well." Serena meant to be polite, but something told her she would like being away from palace intrigue—and also like finding out more about her new husband's way of life.

"No spies here." Rose smiled at her.

"I don't want to be royalty while I am in your home. I don't wish to be treated like a princess," Serena said earnestly. "I want to help, and do the same things you do." She sent a glance to the half apron Rose wore. By no means could Rose be considered homely, though she was considerably more careworn than one might expect royalty to be. She had a graceful way about her, as well as delicate speech. Her demeanor was refined and yet not stiff in any way.

Serena had seen many photos of the late Princess Grace of Monaco. She had never met anyone who reminded her more of Grace than Rose. If some of the cares were worn away from Rose, Serena suspected she would be as gently lovely as Princess Grace had been as she'd grown older.

Perhaps living on a ranch did that to a woman. Serena admired a woman who would sacrifice her beauty for the safety of her children, and the ranch she now oversaw. Would it have been easier for Rose if she'd remained insulated in a princess's world?

But then her sons would have been at risk. Serena well knew the dangers inherent in royal life.

Rose Coleman would have worn sackcloth and starved before she would have let anyone harm her children.

Serena smiled at her new mother-in-law. "I feel very fortunate that I can be here. I know my visit will be all too short."

Cade had been leaning against a wall, his shoulder jammed against the wall as if he held it up rather than accepted its support. Now he stepped away, his interest caught by Serena's words.

Then he turned around and left the room. Puzzled, Serena watched him go.

He did expect her to return to her country, didn't he? It was one thing to leave Balahar so that they could spend some time cementing their marriage. She had merely respected Prince Kadar's wishes in that regard. He had wanted to spend time with her before they…before they—

"You are blushing, Princess Serena," Rose said gently.

"Please. I don't wish to be princess while I am here." Serena made her tone soft so that Rose would not take offense. But she could feel her blush staining her face, and though Rose didn't bring it up again, Serena wondered if she knew she'd been thinking of her son in a physical way. About the two of them sharing marital closeness.

As far as she was from Balahar, Serena felt farther from Cade. The idea of making love with him secretly thrilled her—and yet, she couldn't imagine how they would ever become close enough that he would want to truly take her for his wife.

CADE HELD HIS MOTHER'S stern gaze before glancing at his brother. Mac was distinctly uncomfortable. Mac and Serena had met briefly, and Mac had already expressed his relief at not being the one to marry the princess.

"She's beautiful, Cade," Mac had said sincerely. "But she's not my type. I certainly wouldn't have been happy in this arranged marriage. Not that I mean for you to take care of my responsibility, but—"

"You won't believe this, but I had a chance to back out of the marriage. I could have walked away. Hell, I could have just said that the whole thing was a mistake. But I didn't." He shrugged. "That told me I wasn't immune to the situation."

"My choice of words was poor," Mac said hastily. "I didn't mean to refer to the princess as a responsibility."

"I know you didn't mean that, bro. I just don't want you to feel I did something I didn't want to.

Nobody held a sword to my head, that's for sure. As much as I would have thought someone would have had to before I met Serena.''

"You like her that much?" Mac asked.

"I don't know." Cade had thought that over for a moment. "She's my wife, though, and for some reason, I'm happy about it."

Mac had clapped him on the back. "Congratulations, brother."

Now Rose stared at both of them with searching eyes. "Your out-of-town errand, Mac, was only an excuse, then?"

"A little of both," he replied. "I wanted to see the horses, but I also had to get away to think through my engagement."

"So you didn't know that Kadar planned on marrying Princess Serena under false pretenses?" She glared accusingly at Cade. "Clearly you are totally at fault. I blame you for this lack of respect for the king and myself, Kadar. You don't seem to take the royalty seriously."

"Mother—" Mac began, but Cade overrode him.

"Maybe I haven't taken it as seriously as you would have liked me to," Cade said. "But once I got there, I took the whole matter very seriously. I realized that there had been an understanding, or a misunderstanding on my part, as to my presence in Balahar. Although I had not meant to accept the princess, I would not have backed out at that time.

I know how much this means to you, Mother,'' he said more gently. ''And therefore it is important to me.''

In the hallway, Serena backed away from the door with all the stealth of a palace spy. Not wishing to be waited upon, or to be a trouble to her new family, she had decided to hunt the kitchen up herself—and stumbled upon a private family counsel. Her heart shrank inside her for a reason she couldn't understand immediately.

Never had she dreamed that her husband would not want her for the wifely duties she expected to perform.

Although she didn't know exactly what happened when two people made love, her body had sent her signals she knew meant that she wanted to be alone with him, in his arms.

She understood Cade's wish to save face for his family, but…it hurt more than it should have for a marriage that had been arranged between two strangers. Apparently there was nothing the prince wanted from her, so she brought nothing to the bargaining table—no emotional dowry, in effect. Nothing for her to offer a man?

For a princess used to negotiating as a way of life, this was a very hard fact to accept.

''THIS MARRIAGE WILL HAVE to be annulled,'' Rose announced. ''As much as you may have meant well,

Kadar, you are still not the prince that King Zak believed he contracted for his daughter.''

''No,'' Cade said definitively. ''Mac does not want to be married to the princess.'' He took a deep breath. ''I do.''

''Since when have you wished to be married?'' Rose asked in disbelief.

''Since I laid eyes on Serena.'' Cade looked at his mother with eyes that communicated his sincerity. ''I wouldn't have found a woman I loved on my own, Mother. Being thrown into it is probably the easiest thing I've ever done.''

''I don't believe you can be happy this way, Kadar,'' Rose said. ''Believe me, your nature does not allow you to be happy when you've been pushed into something. You are not one to accept someone's will over your own.''

''No one's will was placed over mine.''

''Mine was. You did this for Mac. You went over there in his place, no doubt thinking to save him the trouble. You find yourself married and now will not admit, even to yourself, that somehow you must extricate yourself from this mistake.'' Rose sighed. ''I do not want to be the one to tell King Zak that his daughter's marriage is not real. That you basically kidnapped her from under his nose.'' Rose sank into a chair. ''Still, this deception must be resolved.''

''I will speak to him. Maybe I can convince King Zak of my sincerity.''

Rose snorted. "He will want more than your sincerity. He may very well ask for your head."

"Why? Why is Mac a better match than me? Serena knew neither of us."

"You are saying he should simply be content to have a man for his daughter?" Rose asked in disbelief. "You or any other, it makes no difference whom?"

"I'm simply saying that I want her, whereas my brother did not. I will take good care of Serena if she feels she can be happy here, and with me."

"Your wishes are not what matter, my son," Rose said tiredly. "I am sorry. It is scandalous that bridegrooms switched places and that negotiations were ignored. It smacks of trickery and is no way to ingratiate one's self with his father-in-law."

"What about her wishes? She may prefer me to Mac." Cade was pretty certain the princess had not been immune to him. At least he hoped she was not.

"These things do not matter where royal marriages are concerned."

"I don't consider myself royally married. We will never live in Balahar. I will not be a ruler."

Rose shrugged. "This is a point on which your wishes and Serena's may not be in harmony. She married with the expectation that she would remain a princess, not become a rancher's wife. It is a very different world than she would expect, Cade. I don't know many women who would want or care to make the transition.''

This was a salient point, Cade silently conceded. Life on a Texas ranch had weeded out many a woman. "I need some time with Serena," he said slowly. "Some time for her to adjust to the ranch before she makes up her mind that she wants to be married to me, and to live here at the ranch." He thought for a few moments. "How long can we hold off King Zak?"

Chapter Six

"It is the first time I ever saw such a spark in Cade's eyes," Rose stated as she sat in the kitchen with her brother, Randy, and his wife, Vi. Rose knew that she could trust these two more than any other with the thorny dilemma confronting her. "My first thought was to call the king immediately. But when I saw Cade struggle not to let me know how much he wanted time for Princess Serena to fall in love with The Desert Rose, I knew he was really asking for time for her to fall in love with him."

"I never thought I'd see the day," Vi said happily. "How did you end the conversation?"

"I agreed to think over whether I could possibly stall King Zak. After all, the situation is beyond highly irregular."

Randy laughed. "Love can make a man do highly irregular things."

Rose noticed the strange look Vi gave her husband. But the moment passed, and Vi's features relaxed into the same pleasant expression she always wore. "How can we help you with this, Rose?"

Always one to ask how she could help, Rose thought gratefully. "I don't know how exactly. Mainly I needed a listening ear to help me decide if I would be doing the right thing if I assisted Cade in this romance."

"Our ears are always available," Randy assured her.

"Separate bedrooms come to mind first," Vi said.

"Separate bedrooms?" Randy queried his wife.

"For Cade and Serena." Vi looked at her husband again, her expression uncomfortable. "Don't you think that's a good idea?"

"I suppose so. Women think about sex differently than men, I know. Will it further the relationship for them to be separated? Seems to me that close quarters is more likely to—"

"Randy!" Vi exclaimed. "You are discussing a princess, remember."

"Who is just the same as any other woman, I would imagine. She will want to be told she is beautiful, and desirable, and—"

"And you think that the only place to do this is in the bedroom?"

Silence met Vi's question. Rose felt a dismayed blush steal over her face. It was clear that her two dearest allies had something to work out between them, although clearly Vi thought that there was more of a problem than Randy apparently did. "Perhaps we should discuss this another time," she murmured.

"Womanly feelings aside, King Zak is not going to want his daughter returned to him in any condition other than that in which she left his palace," Vi said sternly, "should she decide that The Desert Rose—or Prince Kadar—is not to her liking."

"Your point is taken." Rose shifted in her chair. "I may ask the two of you to assist me in some matchmaking if necessary." It suddenly hit her that if anyone was in need of assistance in the love department, it might be Randy and Vi. Which was strange, as they had an upcoming anniversary for which Randy was busily planning a surprise celebration. "And yet perhaps quiet time alone away from court manipulations—or even matchmaking here—might be the better thing."

"Will you want them to stay married?" Randy asked. "Is there a problem with it?"

"I simply do not know how to explain it to the king. He is going to feel that we pulled the wool over his eyes. He may demand that his daughter return at once. With arranged marriages, everything is supposed to be laid out on the table at the beginning. Both sides know what they are getting, and what they are giving. But it is very difficult for me, because I saw the possessive gleam in my son's eyes. Believe me, I would like him to fall in love with a strong, intelligent woman like Princess Serena. I am most impressed with her. I want him to have this marriage, if indeed the two of them are meant for each other.''

''You would be willing to intercede for Cade if you saw that the two of them had mutual ground to build on?'' Vi asked.

''For that I would be willing to intercede,'' Rose admitted. ''I, too, remember the feeling of wanting a love to last beyond all expectations that it should.'' She sighed, her eyes misty with memory. ''It is exquisite beyond all compare when the heart sees its mate in another soul.''

IF HER PRIDE WAS a bit tattered, Serena was determined no one would know it. She would not force Cade to stay in a marriage he had found himself in unexpectedly. She had dreamed of a prince for too long to be unwanted.

She tied on a half apron similar to the one she had seen Rose wearing, and began to peel the potatoes that were set out in a bowl atop the kitchen counter.

''We have a cook,'' Cade said as he came into the kitchen. ''You don't need to do that.''

''I will do it,'' Serena said, ''as your mother did the cooking this afternoon. I saw the apron she wore when we arrived, and I saw her peel a potato. I can do it.''

The glance Cade sent her was puzzled. "My mother likes to cook."

"You think I do not? I like to cook." If she hadn't in several years, and nothing more than popcorn in the dormitory, it was her business to know and not Cade's. Of course, the knife she was using to peel the potatoes did not move as smoothly as it had for Rose, who had cut off the skins in deft, even swirls. The potato seemed to squirm in her hand, an unwilling ally in her show of pride.

"You are going to end up getting a tour of an American emergency room like that," Cade warned. "Let me show you how to do that before you cut yourself."

"Men do not peel potatoes," Serena said, ignoring his request but trimming the vegetable more slowly.

"This man does whatever he likes," Cade said, putting his hands over hers as he stood behind her.

Serena froze. Never had a man stood with such proximity to her! Her father's palace guards, indeed her own servants, would be shocked. "You mustn't stand so close," she said, embarrassed and unable to pay attention to the lesson she was supposed to be receiving as the peels flew into the sink.

He hesitated, the sure stroking ceasing. "I am not standing close, Princess. Not as close as I hope to one day."

She could feel his breath on the back of her neck

where she had pulled her hair up into a long ponytail suitable for kitchen work. Tingles stormed her arms and legs. "You must forgive me, but I am not used to such familiarity."

"You asked me to consummate our marriage," he pointed out. "That seemed very familiar to me."

Heat flushed into her face as she recognized laughter in his tone. "A consummation would be merely an act to legitimize our union."

"Hmm. I don't think that's what you'd say when we were through consummating, as you like to call it, Princess." He put the potato, cleanly peeled, into an empty bowl and reached for another, his hands still on top of hers with every movement.

She stiffened as he began moving her fingers with his in the orchestrated peeling motion that left another potato neatly exposed, its skin lying in the sink in one long, circular ribbon. Her emotions felt like that, easily peeled from her to reveal a virginal heart.

No. She was a princess. She could restrain her emotions as she was accustomed to doing. "What do you think I would call it, Prince Kadar, other than consummation?" she asked icily. "Are you correcting my use of the English language, or bragging like a schoolboy?"

He moved closer, and she felt hot hardness nestle at the base of her spine. She gasped. A gentle, lingering kiss was placed at the back of her neck under her ponytail, and Serena jumped, the potato dropping into the sink as she whirled to face him. She stared up at him, seeing the playfulness in his eyes.

"I would never correct your English, Princess Serena, but I wouldn't brag, either."

He rubbed his palms up over her arms but didn't attempt to kiss her again. She waited for the frenzied dance of her heart to subside so that she could breathe, and yet, she became aware of the presence of his heat at her waist even as she tried to edge back against the sink counter. Her heart danced harder, leaving her unable to do anything but wait for him to move away.

"When I make love to you, Princess," he said huskily, "I want you to call it heaven. I want you to know that you have been loved in a way no other man could make you feel." He pressed his lips to her forehead, her temple, the tip of her nose, lingering just at her cheekbone. "If I make love to you, and you get out of my bed unsatisfied that we have consummated our union, I will put you back in my jet and take you home to Balahar. I make that promise to you."

She shivered, down to her sandaled toes. "I did not mean to insult you...your, um...lovemaking ability, Prince Kadar."

He laughed, moving his lips to her hairline. He warmed her with his nearness, even to the middle part in her hair. "I am not insulted. I am telling you that I want to please you and make you happy, not conform to a legal definition. When I am inside you, we will be man and woman, not prince and princess.''

''Oh, my goodness,'' she murmured. Her mind had never stretched to hearing words like these. Never had her imagination conjured up a romantic relationship. She had always thought in terms of royal lineages, countries bonded through mutually advantageous arrangements, marriages of respect but not necessarily love. ''You are not what I expected in a man at all.''

''I can breed horses all day long if I want to, Serena. Breeding is for animals. Making love is part of marriage.'' He pressed a kiss to the top of her head, at her part. ''I am trying to seduce you.''

''It's working, I think,'' she said on a nervous laugh. ''In the palace, many people say flowery things to earn favor, but I look upon them with scorn. I do not like flowery words, and yet I like yours.''

''You're talking about bootlicking, or in your case, maybe it's sandal-slobbering,'' he told her, brushing his lips against hers. ''I'm romancing you, and glad to hear you like it.''

''I do,'' she said softly. ''Let me romance you.''

He lifted a brow, yet his smile was kind. ''Go ahead.''

She cleared her throat. ''Ah, let me see. Okay. Prince Kadar, when I make love to you, you will know that strands of ephemeral silk tie your heart to mine, and you will never want to break them.''

She leaned up against him, lightly pressing her breasts against his lower chest, and Cade felt his own body igniting.

''And,'' she continued, her eyes full of earnest purpose, ''you will thank the stars that you are not a palace eunuch because you have known such pleasure at my hands.''

He closed his eyes, unwilling to allow her to see the laughter there. His princess's first attempt at seduction should be cherished. ''I can't wait, Serena,'' he said with a smile.

''I am pleased that you are happy,'' she said with a sweet smile for him. ''I appreciate you explaining to me the difference between consummating a marriage and making love.'' She turned back to the sink. ''And I very much appreciate you teaching me how to properly peel potatoes.''

He frowned at his princess's back. Her swift escape from the romantically playful mood they'd been in spoke to her innocence, but it also made him wonder if he'd had Serena under his spell as much as he'd thought, or if she'd merely been pleasing him—humoring him.

Less sure of himself now, Cade said, ''It was no trouble at all. I'll see you at dinner,'' and excused himself from the kitchen. A ride on his favorite horse would give him time to think over his marriage—and his wife. Perhaps he could come up with some answers as to how to convince this beautiful princess that there was a huge difference between consummate and conjugate.

Serena didn't turn around, but a secret smile lifted her lips as the sound of Cade's boots left the kitchen and echoed down the hall. She watched from the kitchen window as he headed toward the stables.

He might have married her to save face for his family, but he was going to relinquish his heart to her. She had dreamed of a prince all her life. Cade might not want to be a prince, but he was going to be hers, by whatever definition he wanted to call it! He wasn't the only one who understood seduction.

She had been raised in a palace, where seduction came in many disguises. His disguise was to think he had helped out his brother and mother by being noble. He was noble, and that was admirable.

However, he didn't yet realize how much he wanted her. She was not going to be merely another duty to him.

And that was where the real seduction would begin.

Unfortunately, she was positive there wasn't much time to put her plan to work. Her father might be unhappy about the prince switch, or Layla might stir up so much trouble at the court that her father would have to send for her to come home with her prince. Sending in a spy with a potion meant that

Layla was ready to take advantage of any holes in the marriage. If Serena's presence—and that of her prince's—was demanded to allay concern about the lack of required pomp and ceremony, Serena knew that Cade would not want to return to Balahar. And that would cause problems. It would be very risky to return if their marriage was still dissolvable.

He wanted an American courtship, a period of dating. "I need to convince him," she murmured to herself as she stroked the skin off the last potatoes, "that a royal match is different. A royal match…needs to be lit or it might get extinguished!"

Chapter Seven

Cade went to the barn in search of his favorite horse, fully intending to ride off the confused mood the princess had put him in. A little seduction should have gone a long way where she was concerned— then why was he feeling he'd had the tables turned on him?

"Whoa, cowboy," Mac told him, busting Cade out of his sour thoughts. "Where are you going in such a hurry?"

"For a ride." Cade pulled down a saddle.

"Somebody shoot your dog?"

Cade looked at his brother. "If you're referencing my mood, I can confirm that it has been in better shape."

"I know it was in better shape before you went into the house. Trouble in the love nest?"

Cade frowned at his brother. "It's a pain in the ass being a prince sometimes."

Mac laughed and tossed him an elaborate silver

and leather bridle. "You've never spent a thought on royalty before the princess brought her vision of loveliness to the ranch."

"I know. That's the problem. I don't much know how to proceed with her."

"I'm so glad it's you and not me, bro, trying to figure out that tangled problem. Although I appreciate you doing me the favor," he said hastily. "I mean, I'm very much aware that it's my boots, er, wedding band you're wearing—"

"Shut up," Cade said, replacing the bridle over a heavy nail in the wall. "I'm not wearing your boots or your wedding band. I wanted her, I've got her, I'm trying to figure out what the hell to do with her."

Mac snickered, earning him a black look from his brother.

"Well, heck. Sometimes Serena looks at me all sweetly, and my insides turn to jelly and I think I'm going to explode. And sometimes she looks at me so knowingly that my insides turn to jelly and I think I'm going to explode."

"Sounds like either way you're going to explode. Your options appear to be limited—and painful."

"You are no help," Cade said curtly. "Wait until it's your turn. You get the next princess Mother conjures up."

"I hope not. I'm hoping that you'll keep her busy with your princess, maybe long enough for me to figure out whether the rodeo life is an appealing option or not.''

"I can just see you leaving The Rose for rodeo." Cade sighed and leaned up against the wall, before picking up a curry brush and beginning to stroke Dakar's powerful body with long, soothing slides of the brush.

"I can't believe one little gal has got you so riled up. Kissin' Cade—isn't that what the girls called you in high school?"

"I hope not." Cade sighed again. "Mac, I know that ranch life is hard. I want Serena to be happy here. It's bad enough that our marriage started off as unfortunately as a dented bucket. For her to be content giving up palace life, she'd have to really love it here."

"You and I do."

"That's different. We never knew any different. She's used to velvet cushions and servants and her every need immediately tended. Here, well, there's none of that. Not even close."

"Guess you're not going to live in Balahar."

"See, that's it," Cade said softly, laying his head against Dakar's shoulder for a moment as he thought. The smell of warm horseflesh came to him, comforting and familiar. A few stalls over, Texas Heat pawed the ground, insisting he get his share of attention. The two stallions couldn't be kept in side-by-side stalls—they would kick apart the wood between them in order to get at each other—and Texas Heat was competitively aware that he wasn't the focus right now. Cade glanced at the stallion. "Slow down, boy. You don't always have to be spoiled rotten." Then he glanced at Mac. "The horses get all the spoiling here, Mac. I'm asking Serena to make a sacrifice, when I'm not willing to do the same. I'd rather be in a wooden box than live in that palace of hers."

Mac shook his head. "I wouldn't want to, either. Remember? That's why you went for me? I didn't even want to make a fast business trip over there."

"So if I want her to be happy enough here to willingly say that she wants to stay at The Desert Rose with me…I don't think the way to make that happen is to throw ranch life at her all at once. And she's in the kitchen wearing an apron and peeling potatoes—after I showed her how not to cut her finger off doing it."

"What made her decide to tackle kitchen duty?"

Cade shrugged, a slight smile lighting his face. "She saw Mother wearing an apron."

"And decided she should emulate her. That shows a willingness on her part to try to like The Desert Rose, Cade. Maybe you're too worried. After all, we have a lot here that is common to a palace. They have sand fleas in the desert, we have biting flies. They have palace politics, we have Mother's matchmaking. They have—"

"I get your point, but life can't be as hard on a palace princess as it is on a cowgirl, can it?"

"It might be," Serena's saucy voice came from the doorway.

Both men straightened to stare at her. She walked toward them slowly, wearing jeans she had to have borrowed from Jessica and a determined smile. "I've got boots on," she told Cade. "I'm ready to ride one of your famous horses. Why don't you show me around this ranch, and give me a chance to decide which is more fun—being a princess or a cowgirl?"

Texas Heat kicked at his stall, tired of being ignored. Ignoring Cade's gape, Serena went to the stall.

"Serena, he may nip you, or worse. Let me get you a pony," Cade said quickly. "I'll saddle one up for you and we can take a nice, leisurely ride around the ranch."

"DR Texas Heat," Serena murmured softly. "Not that you'd need any introduction." She took down a lead rope and, before Cade could stop her, opened the stall. "You're magnificent," she breathed. "Much more impressive than even your pictures," she said to the wary horse. He eyed her and she allowed him to, without extending a hand to him. His great nostrils quivered as he decided whether or not to accept her in his space.

"Serena—" Cade started, but his brother's hand

on his arm stopped him. "She's going to get kicked, or worse."

Mac shook his head. "It would have happened by now. The horse was ready for attention. He senses Serena is going to give it to him."

"She isn't used to riding stallions! She probably rode overfed palace ponies, if they didn't have retainers who rode her horses for her!"

"Serena seems to know what she's about. If she puts the saddle on backward, you'll know she's inexperienced and can step in to help. But give her a chance. She's trying to fit in."

Cade's breath stuck in his throat as he watched the delicate princess woo Texas Heat. The horse drew his head near enough to smell her, giving Cade a fright that Serena might soon lose an ear. But the horse dropped his head a little, satisfied, and Serena slipped the bridle on him without difficulty after inserting the bit.

"Well done," Mac murmured, his voice tinged with admiration.

"So far," Cade grumbled.

"Come on, handsome," she said, leading the horse from the stall. Texas Heat came out, his body proud with shining majesty. "Now, this is a male who needs no words to showcase his attributes," she said to Cade and Mac, while firmly patting the neck muscles. "No need to brag about his prowess. No, this steed knows he has descended from a line of proud royalty, and to pretend otherwise would not be possible. In his very posture, he shows he is a king among his kind.''

She led the horse out from the stable and secured him for saddling, choosing a western saddle for herself and putting it on the horse without assistance. Placing a foot into the stirrup, she neatly vaulted herself into the seat. She stared down at the two cowboys with wicked glee, but her words were aimed at Cade. ''I imagine that when he is sent to visit with a lady, he goes about his business with the sure execution a female expects from a male. Masterfully, enthusiastically, without having to be prodded—and certainly without boastful displays to cover his own lack of confidence.''

Smiling into Cade's astonished eyes, she turned the horse, starting an even canter away from him, before glancing over her shoulder at him for a split second. He could hear her laughter on the breeze.

''What the *hell* was that all about?'' Mac demanded. ''Is the princess trying to tell you something?''

Cade stomped over to swiftly saddle Dakar. ''That I am a recalcitrant prince *and* lover. On the one hand, she is correct. On the other, she, by the stars, is *not*.''

Mac laughed as Cade leaped astride the stallion and none too slowly tore out of the stable. ''I'll call the county fire department,'' he called after his brother, "and warn 'em they're not to worry if they see sparks flying from The Desert Rose!"

IN THE HOUSE, Rose was placing the most difficult phone call of her life. She dreaded telling the king what had transpired so much that her hands shook. Never in her life could she have imagined that Cade would do as he had done.

And yet, he and the princess seemed determined to, if not fall head over heels in instant love, to be satisfied to dig at each other like splinters under skin.

She had never seen Cade act in such a manner. He reminded her of Dakar when a female was brought to him. There was much display of cocky body language, designed to illuminate his magnificent muscles and strong bearing. Rarely had a mare been able to resist the eventual mating, more often than not surrendering to him with submissive posture. Dakar was known for not wasting a rancher's time and money, for he executed his task with speed and potency.

Serena and Cade were, for now, at least in the same corral. Perhaps if she could offer the king something that could soothe the insult Cade had unwittingly visited upon him, something more could come of the marriage than cocky body language and teasing that disguised the attraction between them.

The king would likely want an annulment.

She had little to offer a king that might buy Cade some time with Serena.

"His Highness will speak to you now," the king's adviser said.

"Thank you," Rose murmured.

"Good afternoon, Rose," King Zak said. "It is afternoon in your part of the world, is it not?"

"It is, Your Highness," Rose said respectfully.

"We are related now," the king told her. "Please call me Zak. I was quite pleased with your son, however impetuously he took my daughter from me. I must say that the expediency worked to my benefit, however. No one was the wiser until the deed was accomplished."

"Actually, King Zak," Rose began nervously, "there's a slight problem. Perhaps a large one, actually."

"Don't tell me he doesn't want my daughter!" the king roared.

Rose jumped, gulping nervously. "No, no, that is not the problem, Your Highness. Please do not concern yourself that Serena is anything less than the wonderful princess we expected. Quite the opposite, in fact! She is a star that The Desert Rose never expected to shine upon its humble existence."

"I will hear more of this problem, then. Quickly, please."

Rose's fingers shook on the receiver as she held it to her ear, closing her eyes to pray for the right words. "King Zak, the fault is all my own. My sons have ever been inclined to look after one another. Prince Makin was averse to marrying—anyone at all, although Serena is certainly a jewel to bless a man with many days of joy. Prince Kadar, in seeking to allay his brother's concerns, took it upon himself to stop by Balahar on his way to Saudi Arabia, in order to meet Princess Serena. Apparently, he was confused by palace protocol, and accepted her by accident. So charmed was he by her," Rose continued hastily, "and not wishing to cause her embarrassment, nor to humiliate me, he went through with the marriage."

"My daughter married the third prince? This is not what we agreed upon!"

"No, Your Highness, it is not, and for that, I am dreadfully sorry." Rose's thoughts shifted like sands in the desert wind as she chose her next words carefully. "We could return Serena to you, at once, in the same condition in which she left your palace, which I can promise you is a fact that would be verified easily by a palace physician. Coming home to you with an application for a marriage annulment, however, would most likely bring a stain to her name. Palace gossip would be wicked and intense, as it might appear that her husband did not desire her. Remember, no one knows that Prince Kadar married her instead of Prince Makin, and as they are twins, no one would believe the story if we had to come forward with it. People will say that we fabricated the whole thing.''

"And also that my rule must be weak indeed to allow such a thing to occur under my very nose.''

"Precisely. Which is why I would like to make a counterproposal to you, if I may.''

King Zak hesitated a moment. Rose's fingers tightened on the telephone. The ruler had every right to be outraged, both as a monarch and as a father, and she could not blame him for not wishing to listen to one more word she had to say. For Cade's sake, however, she added a plea.

"Your Highness, please, hear me a little longer. I would like to right this wrong you have suffered.''

After another long moment, he said, "I'm listening, my lady Rose.''

She blinked, both at his kind tone and his choice of words, which brought her to equal status with him. He was giving her the courtesy of a royal with important duties, not the more minor position of an out-of-power queen. Gratitude swelled inside her. "My son and your daughter like each other very much. They came here to protect you. Prince Kadar told your daughter the truth in Balahar. She could have left his side at any moment, revealing him to be an imposter and remaining in her father's home. For the sake of your rule, she went with Kadar, knowing that it was best that a strong marriage bond be portrayed. They came here because already the palace spy had drugged Kadar's drink, hoping to keep him from honoring the princess with a true marriage. An annulment is what I suspect Queen Layla is after, Your Highness, and if Prince Kadar and Princess Serena were unwilling to give it to them, then I humbly suggest that we give them the time to work out the marriage they both seem content to keep.''

"And you have told me that my daughter is still—''

"Yes, Your Highness. My son was unwilling to consummate the relationship under false pretenses, nor did he feel that dancing to the tune of a palace spy and pretender suited him. He would honor your daughter by giving her the time she needs to fall in love with him, to trust him, and more importantly, to be happy married to him.''

"Very unusual for a young man to restrain himself from a bounty when it is laid before him,'' King Zak observed.

A soft laugh escaped Rose. "There is much gnashing of teeth and wearing of pride at The Desert Rose right now, Your Highness.''

"So they do like each other?'' he asked, his tone husky.

"Yes. Very much so, it seems. Enough to want the other to be happy. I would say that it is a very good start.''

"I remember the feeling of wearing my pride and gnashing my teeth," King Zak said thoughtfully.

"As do I," Rose said, her voice wistful.

"Falling in love is a beautiful thing, my lady."

"Yes." She could hardly speak for the pain of remembering just how beautiful it had been for her—before her whole life had been ripped from her by Layla. "I would give this gift to our children, if we can, Zakariyya."

"I think you are right," he suddenly said, his tone authoritative once again. "I am intrigued by your suggestion, and will accept an offer of one Desert Rose foal to make reparation for the pride your son's conduct has cost me."

"You are more than generous, King Zak."

"How many were you going to offer me?"

Rose smiled. "The very best next three The Desert Rose produced."

"You got off lightly," the king said. "Shrewdness is appealing in a woman, for when her beauty fades, she still has that attribute left to her. I will be anxiously awaiting an update in one week's time. If I do not hear from you, I will come for my daughter myself. This will cause me bad humor. And two weeks' time is all I can allot for the prince and princess to do more than posture and crow at each other. Surely that is long enough for a man to know his own mind. Tell Prince Kadar I am displeased that he deceived me. Tell him that I will cut off his hand if he compromises my daughter before she decides she will be his. Tell him the Balahar royalty does not need to send to Texas for a stud—we have plenty of young men here who would pay handsomely to wed my daughter. A man who comes in and steals my daughter out from under my nose in the cover of night in his jet should be good for a couple of grandchildren—er, royal heirs.''

"Yes, Your Majesty,'' Rose said, knowing that the pompous tone covered his pleasure with the situation.

"I will send you some pictures of the wedding. It was a small, impromptu affair, of course, but you will enjoy seeing the two of them in royal wedding attire.''

"Yes, I will. Thank you. Your kindness is more than I deserve.''

"Your time away from court has taken nothing from the sweet manner with which you are trying to assuage me, Rose. I can see why your husband found you to be such a fit mate, and no doubt an excellent queen.''

"Thank you,'' she said, surprised by the compliment.

"Wisdom, diplomacy and a loving spirit are rare in a woman,'' the king said quietly. "I miss them.''

Whatever gift she had with words flew out the window at his bereft words.

"I will await your phone call,'' he suddenly commanded. "Do not make me wait for word of progress. Goodbye."

"Goodbye," she murmured, knowing he had already hung up the phone.

Chapter Eight

"Serena, wait!"

The urgent, angry call of Cade's came to her, despite the canter she had set the horse to. Hearing hoofbeats behind her, she encouraged Texas Heat into a gallop toward lush, green pastureland. Texas Heat sensed Dakar behind him, and his proud spirit refused to let himself be caught. Determined to win at all costs, he galloped hard and true. Serena laughed. "Go, go, go!" she urged him.

Seeing a creek winding up ahead, she wondered how Texas Heat would react to the change in landscape. Until now, she had been content to give him his head, knowing that his winner's spirit was operating in full. A body of water changed matters, however; she dared not risk injuring an excellent horse by asking it to cross water if it wasn't used to doing so. This horse was used for show purposes and for stud, and maybe had rarely seen a creek. She would have to accept that here the race finished,

Serena realized; here she would have to face an angry prince.

Just as she prepared to command the horse to slow, powerful muscles beneath her saddle tensed, launched and carried her over the creek. She gasped, aware that the horse had known to jump the creek at a narrow pass, as the hooves landed neatly on gray clay, never missing more than a beat as Texas Heat continued his eager quest for the crown of champion.

''Serena!'' Cade barked.

She glanced back to see that Dakar had jumped the creek at the same place. ''You are going to get winded, my mighty warrior,'' she told the horse. ''We have made our point and won the trophy, so please, allow the sore losers to catch up with us. We must not injure their pride altogether.''

Bit by bit, Texas Heat slowed to a joyous gallop, then to a canter for a few hundred feet, and then to a reluctant yet showy prancing walk, as if to say, ''Ha! Did you enjoy my long tail waving at you like a banner you couldn't catch!''

''You could have hurt yourself!'' Cade told her, coming alongside her horse. ''Not to mention Texas Heat!''

''Your champion is fine. Thirsty, but fine. Let me cool him down before you allow your hot head to tell me off.'' Slowly she turned to take Texas Heat in a wide circle, once, twice, three times. Then she slid from his back and, pulling the reins over his head so that she could hold them, walked him to the creek so he could drink. She didn't let him drink too much, just enough to slake the dryness from his mouth, then led him to a tree where she looped the reins around a branch. "Graze if you will, mighty warrior," she told him. "You deserve it."

She caught begrudging admiration in Cade's eyes before he turned Dakar, mimicking her actions before choosing a tree far enough away from Texas Heat that there would be no trouble. The horses were too tired to be competitive right now, but they were healthy and would rally back all too soon. Seating herself on a flat patch of grass beside the creek, she waited for her prince's hot words to flow over her.

And no doubt they would, she thought, watching him stride toward her. Wearing jeans that melded to strong thighs, boots that gave him an appearance of strength, and a denim shirt open to mid-chest, she had to admit that he wasn't the robed sheikh prince of her dreams. But he *was* sexily handsome.

"Cowgirl," she told him as he stood beside her, not deigning to sit in order that he might show her his temper.

"What?"

"I believe it is more fun to be a cowgirl than a princess." She glanced up at him with teasing eyes, pushing a strand of chestnut hair behind her ear. "Isn't that what you and your brother were discussing—whether I could be happy at The Desert Rose?''

He'd gotten so lost in the combat of the race, he'd forgotten what had set it off in the first place, Serena realized with a smile.

''I don't want to talk about that right now,'' he instructed impatiently. ''I want to discuss some basic ranch rules. I had to learn some rules when I was at your palace—namely, don't drink anything handed me by palace servants, and censor my words in case I might be overheard. Here the survival skills are different, Princess. I don't want you riding the stallions.''

Serena's eyes went wide. ''Were you not proud of my riding skill, my prince?''

''I was. I want to see a helluva lot less of it.''

She frowned at his growl. ''As you wish.'' Getting to her feet, she pulled off the boots Jessica had lent her, and rolled up the borrowed jeans as close to her knees as she could manage with their narrow cut. Stuffing her socks down into the boots, she hurled them across the creek to land in the soft grass before wading into the creek at approximately the point where Texas Heat had jumped.

''What are you doing?''

''I am returning to the house,'' Serena replied, not bothering to look back.

''Serena!''

Now she did turn. ''Yes?''

"You will not leave in some princessy snit. We are here because of you, and so you will not run away from me again. I am not in the mood to chase you."

"I am not in the mood to be chased, so I am glad we can agree on this matter, my prince." Without another word, she walked into the water up to her hips. "Are there snakes in this water?"

"Not that I have seen. Come back here at once."

"I will not. You are standing in a bed of something your mother instructed me as necessary to be avoided, and you will be soon joining me, if she is as wise as I believe she is."

He glanced down at his boots, suddenly realizing he was standing in a bed of fire ants. "Damn it!" he shouted, hopping to jerk his boots off and tossing them aside. "Damn it!" he exclaimed again before managing an impressive leap into the water.

"Your mother was right," Serena said with a grin after the splash subsided.

He narrowed his eyes at her, working furiously at his jeans legs to make certain the ants had not crawled up farther than he anticipated. "You would not be laughing if you had gotten stung."

"I was not so foolish as to stand on dangerous ground," she rejoined, moving to a deeper part of the creek so that she could sink into it up to her neck. "This feels wonderful," she said on a sigh. "Just like the indoor pools of the palace."

She felt his eyes upon her, white-hot with interest and male perusal. Ever so innocently, she ducked under the water, coming up with her hair slicked behind her and her gaze meeting his with feminine allure. "So," she said softly, "you do not think me capable of riding a stallion? You would give me a tamer mount?"

His denim shirt was wet and outlined strong muscles of a chest and torso as well defined as any soldier's in her father's army. Serena admitted to herself that she had never seen a male like Prince Kadar. He stood still, like a master-carved statue, watching her in a hawklike manner. She shivered, enjoying the sensation of being his prey.

He is my husband. He could possess me whenever he wished.

She shivered again, harder, and lowered her gaze.

"I would not give you a tamer mount. I would give you one that suits your needs, and which I could trust to bear someone whom I would not care to see injured."

Her gaze flew upward to meet his glowing eyes.

Even the water stilled between them as they stared at each other, measuring. Gauging the moment, the intensity, the level of their relationship.

I want him to want me, Serena thought to herself. *As a man wants a woman. Royalty has almost always slept alone, secluded by the crown it wears. I want more.*

"Swim with me, Prince Kadar," she asked softly. "I would enjoy you teaching me the many things your mother has not yet had time to tell me about The Desert Rose."

His gaze stayed on hers for a moment. She stayed under water to her neck, keeping the invitation as sexless as possible.

"You cannot hide from me," he told her huskily. She blinked at him.

"I know you are hiding behind a veil of sudden acquiescence."

"Do not tear the veil from me, then, my prince, as it is a hard veil for me to wear."

"Me, as well. I sense that you have changed the subject from stallions to my mother's teachings to tell me that you will ride whichever of the horses you choose at any time."

"Oh, no," she said, shaking her head at him, although her gaze did not move from his. "I will ride the mount my husband chooses for me. I am touched by his concern for my safety."

He neared her, causing ripples to splash up between them as he clasped her to him, seating her legs around his waist. "I will not give you a tame mount, Serena. I know you would not be content with that. We have enough horses at The Desert Rose that you may choose from many which will take care of the princess I would not wish harmed."

Leaning his forehead against hers, he gazed into

her eyes. She felt her prickly pride melt a little, and allowed her arms to ring his neck. "I wanted you to catch me," she whispered.

"I have never ridden so hard in my life."

A slight smile touched her lips, and then his.

"It was a prize worth the race," he told her. "I am impressed with your seat."

"I am glad," she said shyly. "I was afraid you'd be angry."

"I was. I am. I will be if you ever pull that stunt again, cowgirl."

She leaned her cheek against his. "You have goose pimples along the back of your neck."

"You have them on the front of your neck," he told her, holding her back a bit so that he could examine them. "The water is too cold for you. I can't let you catch a cold."

"I am not cold in your arms." She pulled away from him, floating onto her back so that the sun's waning rays would warm her body. "But if you are cold, you do not have to swim with me."

He grabbed her, pulling her back to him easily since the water made her lighter than ever. "You are cold," he said on a growl in her ear. "You are not wearing a bra, and it is plain to see that you are *very* cold. Why are you not wearing anything under that shirt? Do you want the ranch hands to go nuts?"

She blushed as he locked her legs back around his waist as they had been before—only this time there was something hard and rigid in the spot between his legs. "I could not borrow something as personal as underwear," she confessed. "A brassiere seems quite personal to have to ask for. We left in quite a hurry, and since we were sneaking away, I packed little besides some jewels and makeup. Much more baggage would have been suspect had we been seen. So I only have one brassiere, and it is in the wash."

His eyes went intensely dark as his gaze left her eyes, sliding to take in the hard peaks of her nipples clearly lined by the soft, wet material of her shirt.

"I do not want to disturb the ranch hands, but it would be my pleasure if you found me irresistible," she confessed. "Perhaps I should never wear a bra."

"I will lock you away like a princess in a tower if you do," Cade warned. "I cannot believe you have been walking around without a bra at The Desert Rose."

"American denim is much heavier than anything I wear in the palace. I have not been indiscreet."

"No, you have not. I have been…blind." He touched a palm to her breast, feeling the weight of it in his hand, outlining it with his fingers. "To have treasure like this so close by and not see it crying out to be found—" He broke off, slowly unbuttoning the top three buttons of her shirt, so that the material floated open, gaped by the water. Her breasts lay fully open to view, and Serena's breath caught at the expression on Cade's face. His fingers stroked her, lightly pinched her nipples, and the hunger in his eyes grew, almost as if he were mesmerized by rare, beautiful jewels. She had seen that look on other men's faces when they beheld the jewels of the palace—but Kadar's hunger was all for her. He sucked a nipple into his mouth, and she gasped, holding on to the back of his head, thrilling at the feeling of his dark hair between her fingertips. *I like being a cowgirl,* she thought wildly. His other hand reached to squeeze her other breast and she moaned. Licking and kissing assailed the other nipple and she edged toward the hardness in his jeans, a siren's cry she didn't want to escape.

"My husband, please let us consummate our marriage. I do not think I can stand the torment of not knowing what further pleasures you can teach me!"

As if the water had turned icy cold around them, he pulled away, staring at her.

"What? What is it?" she asked.

Slowly he shook his head. He reached out again and she held completely still, thinking he meant to bring her the wild pleasure she felt when he kissed her breasts. Disappointment scored her when he began to button her shirt.

"Why have you stopped?"

He placed his lips against her forehead, withdrawing his lips just as quickly. "Let me get you home and dry you off," he said, taking her by the hand

and leading her from the creek. "I will have Mother take you into town tomorrow for clothes, and will assign a stable boy and horse to you for your needs."

"But I—"

Without a word, he untied and mounted Dakar. Then Cade pulled Serena up behind him.

"I can ride Texas Heat home—"

"You will not ride the stallions, please, Serena. Your father would not want his daughter hurt while she is here in Texas," Cade commanded her in a stern voice.

"But you will have to come back to get him!"

"I will have a ranch hand drive me out so that I can ride him back. The horse will be fine."

He circled the horse wide and then jumped at the narrow point of the creek again. Serena held on to her husband's back, her heart in shreds.

"Will you ever consummate our marriage?" she asked as they slowly cantered home.

"That was the purpose of bedeviling me into following you, I guess," Cade replied. "You threw out the challenge of the steed who delivered what was expected of him, and I suppose I chased you down with the notion to make you eat your words. I'm a reluctant prince, and I'm a reluctant lover right now. That's just the way it is."

Serena raised a disdainful eyebrow at his imperious tone, the princess in her not liking that one little bit. She wasn't going to argue with him, however. Sweet sugar cubes were much more likely to bring the potent, commanding stallion to her than were hot demands.

With a mental shrug, she pressed her breasts against his back. The cold, wet denim they both wore accentuated the hardness of her nipples, and she made certain he felt that for the rest of the ride home.

By the stiff manner in which he reached behind him to help her slide off the horse at the barn, before glaring at her with black eyes as he wheeled Dakar for a fierce ride across the pasture, she was fairly certain sweetness was a far better coin with which to repay his arrogant words.

Mac eyed her disheveled, wet appearance with a grin as she walked past the barn toward the house. She was careful to keep her long hair in front of her, concealing from view that which Cade had found so fascinating.

"So, how did you like the tour of the ranch?" he called.

She gave him a saucy stare but didn't stop walking, knowing he was laughing at her bare feet and soaked clothes. "You will have to ask your brother how he enjoyed being tour guide."

Laughter followed her comment. Jessica and Rose met her at the door as she went inside.

"What happened to you, Serena?" they exclaimed.

"Prince Kadar and I have disagreed," she said simply. "On many things, but some more concerning than others."

"Oh, my," Rose said, her face crestfallen. "Is there anything I can do to help?"

Serena shook her head. "Not unless…you know where I might purchase suitable undergarments for Texas."

"Suitable…undergarments?" Jessica echoed.

Serena felt her face blush uncontrollably. "Prince Kadar is offended by my lack of…a…brassiere," she said, her embarrassment full and complete now.

"I didn't realize you did not have…suitable things, Serena. This can be remedied at once," Rose said.

Taking in her shamed face, Jessica said, "I'm not certain that my cousin was offended by her lack of anything, Aunt Rose."

The two crossed gazes before Rose stared back at Serena. Slowly her eyes traveled every inch of the princess. "I think you have perceived something I had missed, Jessica. If you will allow me, Princess, I believe I know just the place where Jessica can take you before dinner. If you will go with her, I promise you that offended is the last thing Prince Kadar will be the next time he sees you."

"Thank you, Mother Rose," Serena said gratefully. "I'll change into dry clothes and be ready in fifteen minutes."

Rose watched as the princess ascended the stairs. "Take my credit card, which is in my purse, with you, Jessica, and please make certain that the princess is outfitted with the proper undergarments my son wishes she wear. Daytime trousseau she most certainly needs, nothing practical at all, and for night, be certain to pick up something that can be seen through as easily as glass and yet will tantalize a young prince who needs a little encouragement to tend his wife. I'm pretty certain King Zak would approve of my methods," she said with a satisfied smile.

"This is going to be fun," Jessica said with glee. "I can't wait to see the expression on Cade's face when Serena shows him her souvenirs from Victoria's Secret!"

Chapter Nine

A relaxing meal after the invigorating afternoon swim with his princess was what he needed, Cade decided, surveying the table with satisfaction. His vixen of a wife had given him a good run for his money with her wild chase on horseback. Then she had followed up that stunt by watching him stand in an ant bed, necessitating his jumping into the cold stream.

He refused to even think about what the cold water had done to his vow of restraint. Who would have thought his pampered princess would have been lacking proper undergarments? Hours later, he still felt need for her burning inside him.

"Maybe I will have wine tonight," he told the cook as she moved past his place with the wine pitcher, knowing that he didn't drink it.

"You don't drink wine," she commented with a roll of her eyes, ignoring him.

Soothing his raging mind was paramount; wine

might help dull the panic his wife seemed to visit upon his desire. "Wine would go well with the steak I smell grilling," he prevaricated. But that made him think about a wife determined to inflame his senses past anything he'd ever experienced. He needed a clear head to deal with her. "Never mind," he said curtly. "Maybe wine is a bad idea."

The cook snorted, disregarding him as she continued filling the goblets.

He drummed the table with his fingers, waiting for the rest of his family to enter the dining room. They weren't usually this late. Footsteps sounded on the stairs and he relaxed a little. At last! If they'd hurry up, he could get to the chow, and after today's activities, he was starved.

But the only person who walked into the room was Serena, and his appetite for food went right out the window.

A strapless ice-teal evening gown hugged her waist and fell in a straight satiny shimmer to her ankles. Matching sandals with rhinestone-encrusted thin heels peeped from beneath the dress as she walked toward the table. Her chestnut hair was pulled into a tousled upsweep, which gave him a clear view of beautiful shoulders and carried his gaze along the natural slope of her body to her bust-line.

As far as he could tell, Serena had decided against borrowing a brassiere from either of the ladies in the house—and further, planned to flaunt her lack of one.

Did she think he was made of stone?

Before he could voice the question aloud, he saw two smiling faces peeking around the corner of the dining room—his mother, and Jessica.

A setup. They'd dolled up his wife on purpose, and he was no match for their seductive staging. He was outgunned—and none too happy about it.

"Serena," he said, his voice low. "Would you mind joining me upstairs in my room for a moment?"

She stared at him in surprise before a pleased smile dawned on her face. "It would be my earnest pleasure, husband."

He rose and held out a hand, indicating that she should precede him from the room. As they passed into the hall, he nodded at his mother and cousin. "Good evening, Mother," he said smoothly. "You're looking well. Jessica," he said politely, with another nod, before following his wife's swaying, shimmering backside up the stairs.

"I think it's safe to say we'll be eating with only Mac tonight," Rose said happily. "We'll have to remember to send the honeymooners up a tray!"

"Honeymooners," Jessica repeated thoughtfully. "Do you realize Cade and Serena haven't had a honeymoon?"

A worried frown settled on Rose's face. "I hadn't

thought about it, but it's something to consider if—''

Upstairs, a door closed with a decided thud. The sound reverberated in the hall downstairs.

With dismay, Rose and Jessica stared at each other. The sound hadn't been one of two lovers sneaking off for a rendezvous.

''We may have to consider rigging some type of honeymoon if those two can't work out the kinks in the next two weeks,'' Rose said authoritatively. ''I promised the king they'd be cooing like lovebirds if we gave them enough time, and his version of enough is fourteen days!''

CADE STARED at the lovely woman in front of him, her hands locked together at her hips as if she feared he might devour her whole. He reminded himself that this princess talked a good game, but she was a virgin—and no doubt thought that his family's machinations had finally brought him to heel.

They had done nothing but push him further from their apparent goal. ''Serena,'' he said softly, ''you look lovely tonight.''

She visibly relaxed. ''Thank you. I do want to please you, my prince.''

''You do. Although I have to admit, I'm somewhat uneasy about you walking around without...''

''Without, Prince Kadar?''

He swallowed. "Without that which we discussed this afternoon!"

"Oh…" she said, her tone dawning with realization. "You need not worry about your wife walking around the ranch without proper clothing anymore."

She reached to her side and undid a side zipper, allowing the sheath of ice-teal to fall to the floor in a fast sigh that seared Cade's nerves like a razor stroke. "That is not a bra," he said hoarsely, staring at the white, sequined garment that hugged her full breasts, lined her sleek waist and all but bared her femininity to his starved gaze. Satiny garters held up sheer white stockings on legs that were slim and fit. Her feet tucked into the delicate teal sandals with rhinestone heels topped off a vision of delicate innocence—and sensual promise. "That is not a bra," he repeated dumbly, feeling somehow as if he'd been tricked.

"It is. I am covered where you want me covered," she said, touching her chest area for emphasis. "This is called a merry widow, although I must say I would much rather call it a merry bride. Or a merry wife. I like the sound of that better." She smiled at him. "Would you like to examine the fabric, my prince?"

His mouth dried out. "I—"

"I wonder if they have anything called a merry husband," she said, slowly walking toward him.

"I'm not feeling very merry at this moment," Cade said. "Serena, I would like to examine every inch of that…that, but I cannot," he said on a rush, backing up slightly so that she halted in her tracks. "We need to get to know each other better."

"I am trying!"

He shook his head. "There's more to marriage than sex. We haven't talked over any of the points of what we're going to do with our lives."

She frowned at him. "Your cousin says you are much more for talking than Mac. Perhaps you are all talk and no action."

"I most certainly—" He stopped, sniffing out the trap in her words. "Be that as it may," he continued, ignoring the barb, "that's a perfect example of why we need to get to know each other better before we make love."

"You're afraid I'm not going to like you," Serena said. "And then I'll be stuck with you because I can't go home dishonored."

"Yes," Cade said with enthusiasm. "That's exactly it. And it's not just me, it's the ranch. Life in Texas is very different from what you've been used to."

"I've heard all these arguments," Serena said, her chin lifting. "I am ready for my husband to favor me. After all, how will I know if I truly like you unless you make love to me?"

His jaw dropped, her angle one he hadn't anticipated.

She paced the room, her backside gleaming and round underneath a shadow of lace as she did, shattering his concentration. He direly wished she would put her evening gown back on!

"How many women have you favored?" she demanded, turning to face him.

"What?"

"How…many…women…have you favored?" she asked slowly and loudly, as if he were near-deaf. "Can you recall them?"

"Of course I can!" he said, wondering where his princess's devious mind was heading. "If I understand your terminology correctly to mean how many women have I made love to."

"Yes. That is what I want to know."

"Some."

She raised her brows. "Some?"

He nodded. "A few."

"A few."

He nodded again.

"And where are they now, these women that you favored?"

"I don't know!"

"So you knew, once you had made love with them, that you really did not like them. Otherwise they would be somewhere around The Desert Rose. I have not seen any of your women."

"I have no harem here."

"So you did not really like them for very long."

"I suppose not."

"Then how do you expect me to know whether I like you if we do not make love? How does a woman know whether she likes a man or not unless she has experienced the ultimate pleasure with him?"

"Trust me, you would experience the ultimate pleasure with me, Princess."

She crossed her arms, which sent her breasts mounding up over the top of the merry widow, filling him with a desire to investigate and conquer that undiscovered territory. "Yes, so you say, but we have already determined that you are a man who boasts but not necessarily acts upon his word."

He kept his mouth shut now, his gaze simmering on her full lips before locking on to the determined expression in her eyes.

"This does not bode well for you," she assured him. "I am thinking now that perhaps you are right. Maybe I won't want to be married to you once we have made love."

"That isn't what concerns me!"

She held up a hand, showing a light plane of underarm that he found surprisingly sexy. So far, he couldn't see a centimeter of his wife he didn't find charming.

"All the women vie for the privilege of Prince

Sharif's bed,'' she said, holding her pose, one hand gesturing to emphasize *all the women.*

"I am not interested in hearing about Prince Sharif,'' Cade growled.

She ignored him. "There is not a woman who does not pray to Allah for an invitation to his bed. To be thusly invited shows most favored status, and improves one's position in the harem.'' Her gaze held his. "I have not been so favored by my own husband. It is humiliating.''

Cade's jaw dropped for a second, before he reached out to grab his wife and pull her down onto his lap as he sat on the bed. "Serena, this is not a harem. You have no worry about position here. As my wife, you are special. You are not losing face in any way, and besides which, no one can know that we're not up here right now, uh, having favors with each other.''

She laughed shyly at his bungling of the term. "You do not understand. A woman who cannot please her husband might as well pack her small bag and get back on a plane.''

"I do not want you to go, unless you want to go. More than anything, I want you to be happy at The Desert Rose, and be my wife.'' With one finger, he traced the soft skin revealed above the merry widow. "Trust me, Serena, if we decide to stay married, I would need only you. I would stay in your bed the way a faithful soldier stays in your palace's army.''

She smiled hesitantly. "Even the most obedient soldier falters from time to time."

He kissed the white skin of her shoulder. "Are you saying my weapon would be laid down? I assure you that would not be the case. It's not, even now."

She started, her eyes wide as she realized she was sitting very near the subject of their discussion. "You do want to favor me, then?"

He pressed his face between her breasts and traced her bottom with his hands. "I want to make love with you, yes. And I promise you that you won't have to worry about not liking me after we've made love."

She snuggled against his neck. "I was truly teasing you, my prince. I was trying to be very American and progressive."

"You could give a guy a complex like that," he said, nipping at the curve of her collarbone. "I've never had a woman mention that she didn't like me after the fact. I may have to call and ask them."

She tugged at the hair on his nape. "I will cut off your finger if it so much as dials the number of one girlfriend."

He chuckled. "That doesn't sound very much like a woman who's grown up around harems and understands a man's needs."

"Women can be spiteful in the harem, although they don't cut off anyone's hands, usually," she said, nipping at his earlobe. "However, in America

I have decided to do as the Americans do. You may not have a harem.''

''You're kind of bossy for a princess,'' he said, standing her back on her feet so that he could slide the satin gown back over her head.

''You're rather more like a mule than a stallion, my prince,'' she shot back. ''I *will* be a merry wife one day.''

''That reminds me,'' he said, kissing her forehead. ''Are you going to wear that merry thing every day?''

She stepped back from him and went to the mirror, sending him a saucy smile in the image. ''I promised to obey my prince about the brassiere thing, didn't I? Your cousin took me to Victoria's Secret today, and I now own enough undergarments to make certain that for as long as I stay here, my husband's wishes are done. Every day, in a different style, and a different color.''

''Remind me to send Jessica back to college,'' he said on a groan. ''Maybe she should take up some advanced studies to keep her from influencing my wife.''

He followed her from the room, and down the stairs to join the family in the dining room. However, at the doorway, Serena stopped, causing him to bump into her delicious backside.

''Whoa,'' he said, reaching out to steady her. ''What's wrong?''

"I have to call my father," Serena said suddenly. "Please make my excuses to your family for missing the evening meal with them."

And then she tore back up the stairs, her teal skirt held in her hands so that she could hurry. Cade stared after her. "Missing the meal with them was their intention," he said to no one.

What had made his princess vanish like day before night?

"ONE MOMENT, Princess Serena, I will get Prince Sharif for you," her father's chief adviser said. "Your father is at a meeting in the city, or I am certain he would want to speak with you as well."

"That's all right. Prince Sharif is fine for now. Thank you." Her mission of seduction could best be answered by the man who had a many women vying for his favors. She needed to know how long it took before a man could consider that he knew a woman well enough to make love to her; this was not a question she could ask of any females in the palace harem. The gossip would be enormous and scathing that she could not lure her prince into bed.

No, Prince Sharif was the appropriate person to give her the man's perspective on love.

"Hello, my sister," he greeted as he came on the line.

Familiar feelings of love and closeness rushed

into her at the sound of Sharif's voice. "How good it is to hear you, Sharif!"

"And you, as well. The palace is not the same without you."

"Perhaps I am not the same without the palace," Serena said quietly.

"You are not happy with Prince Kadar?" Sharif asked quickly. "He is not kind to you? I will come at once and cut his—"

"No, no, no!" Serena exclaimed. "I mean that maybe I am not all my prince thought I would be once he brought me to his home."

Sharif hesitated. "My sister, you are all he thought you were and more, I am sure. What makes you have these worries? It is his job to make you feel secure in a land where you are unfamiliar, and secure among his people."

Serena laughed. "His people are kind and generous. They have included me as one of their own. His land is different, but I like it. No, Sharif," she said, her voice lowered, "my problem is a delicate one."

"I will help you if I can, but perhaps you should call the harem and speak to—"

"No. I cannot do that. I need to know how a man thinks, not how a woman thinks who is trying to please a man. My prince seems immune to that."

"Ah. I understand."

Serena's eyebrows flew up. "You do?"

"Absolutely. He is bored."

"Bored?" She didn't like the sound of that at all.

"Yes. He has had many women who tried to possess him. They have all tried their tricks on him. He is weary of women's wiles. So you must forget whatever you learned in the harem."

"Well, it wasn't much," Serena muttered. "The women were careful around my ears."

"All the better then. Anyway, American people are very different about this marriage thing. This one-man, one-woman situation is very trying. You must be all the more captivating, without actually seeming to be trying to captivate him, of course."

"But how? He won't even...even—" Serena broke off, blushing. "Our marriage could be annulled at any moment," she finished on a dismayed whisper.

"Has he said that is what he wants?"

"No. He says he wants to wait until I know my own mind."

"Allah be praised for bringing such a man to my sister," Sharif said joyfully, "even if I cannot fully comprehend such restraint."

"You would not show such restraint with your bride, then?"

"Certainly not. However, I do not expect to love my wife. I will make a political alliance with no expectation of love. Harems are for pleasure—marriage is for duty. Yet it is clear that your prince has fallen in love with you.''

''In love…with me?'' Serena echoed in disbelief.

''Why else would he care whether you know your own mind or not? Women are not supposed to know their minds.''

''Oh, Sharif,'' Serena said on a moan. ''You have had the luxury of a harem too long.''

''Actually, I have not visited the harem in a great while. I tell you I am restless, and it is true. This is why I think I sympathize with your prince. It would be far more satisfying to find a woman with whom I wanted more than simply a night of pleasure— although I will admit that the nights of pleasure here are satisfying. It's just that I find myself longing for something more.'' Sharif paused a moment. ''Anyway, you are a beautiful, talented woman. Of course he wants his wife to be happy with him. What has he got to compare to a palace?''

''I wondered that at first, but there is so much here that you would find it every bit as beautiful as the Balahar jewels.''

''Will you want to stay there forever, then?''

''Well, we have not discussed that,'' Serena said carefully. ''Prince Kadar has no interest in succession to the throne, so…I think I would have to stay here forever.''

''You see why he wants you to know your own mind, then,'' Sharif said softly. ''It is bad to have an unhappy wife. He wants you to choose him and his palace of your own accord." A chuckle filled Serena's ear. "I admit that I wasn't sure I liked your prince when he came here."

"Strange. He doesn't want to talk about you much, so you two somehow started off on the wrong path."

"It is near impossible to have two stallions in the same corral," Prince Sharif said, and Serena could hear the smirk in his voice. "I was none too pleased to discover that your husband was not the prince he claimed to be, either. However, Layla has had her spy turning the palace upside down trying to discover your whereabouts, so I decided that Prince Kadar had done the right thing, even if it did end up costing him an Arabian foal. We have certainly gotten the better end of this transaction. And people say it is a pain to deal with Americans! I say it has been very lucrative, and since you seem to be in his eternal favor, satisfying as well."

"What are you talking about? What foal did marrying me cost him?"

"Oh, not marrying you. His mother, the former Queen Rose, has paid a tribute of a Desert Rose Arabian foal to our father to make up for the dishonor of her son's kidnapping of you from our home."

"It was not kidnapping!"

"To make up for his stealthy departure, then,"

Prince Sharif amended, though his tone clearly indicated that the former verb stated his opinion better. "Actually, the foal was really to soothe Father into allowing you to stay in Texas for fourteen days, in order for your prince to decide whether you would stay."

"Stay! Fourteen days! How do you know this?"

"Our father has told me this. He is well pleased with his end of the bargain."

"I am not a prize to be bargained," Serena said hotly. "I will not be returned in fourteen days if my husband decides he doesn't want me. I am not a defective purchase to be returned!"

Sharif laughed. "I think you will not return, unless it is by your choice. What you have told me about Prince Kadar shows that he is willing to pay a foal in order to give his wife time to know her own mind, even if she shouldn't know it—" he began in a teasing tone. "No, that's not right. It's your heart he wants you to know, Serena. He is trying to be gentle with you, like a mare who has never worn the saddle before. Perhaps you should give his method some thought, sister. After all, you admit that you will miss the palace, and that he does not wish to rule. These are not small things you are giving up."

"I do not think he is in love with me," Serena demurred. "I think he is not attracted to me, or else he would wish to do what he could to keep me here, such as showing me his favor.''

"He is trying. It's just different from what you have known here.''

"I do not think I like a horse being exchanged for fourteen days with me,'' Serena said warily. "I feel bartered. Is that what love is supposed to feel like?''

"Rose offered the foal to make up for the behavior of her son. Prince Kadar had no knowledge of the offer. I only know because Father said this. It is not so unusual, Serena, and Father was well pleased by her gesture. To be honest, I think her knowledge of royal manners and protocol has caught Father's attention in some mysterious way. Anyway, you called for my advice, and I am ready to give it to you now.''

He hesitated, and Serena impatiently blurted, "I am listening!'' She heard another chuckle.

"Try to become as much a part of his life as you can. What he loves, you must love.''

"That would be his family,'' she said thoughtfully. "And his horses.''

"Then you see that the task in front of you is minor. You know how to honor family, and you know much about horses. As you are camping out there disguised as a peasant, you should be able to spend much time in the barns.''

"Cowgirl, not peasant," she murmured. "I'm wearing jeans and boots during the day."

"And at night?"

"We sleep in different rooms."

"Then that is something you must seek to change. I do not say make him do that which he seems unwilling to do at this time. However, there is much comfort in a woman who knows how to lie upon a man's chest quietly, as a soul mate, without demanding or asking for attention all the time. I would like a soul mate," he said wistfully.

"My brother, are you all right?" Serena asked. "I am beginning to worry about you."

"Do not. Make your fourteen days count carefully," the prince instructed. "The time will pass swiftly, so be certain that you take advantage of this peace the prince has paid for with a prize foal, and utilize it to your advantage."

"Thank you, my brother," she said softly. "Your words have brought me courage and insight, as I knew they would."

"Of course," Prince Sharif agreed cheerfully. "Have I not been trained to be a wise and fit ruler?"

Serena laughed at her brother's ego, already snapped back into place and all discussion of soul mates forgotten by him. "You are wise and fit," she agreed, "if not humble."

"Remember," he said, his voice full of good humor, "a time of quiet is when two people can do the most communicating, even without saying a word. I must go now, my sister. Goodbye.''

He rang imperiously off the line without waiting for her to thank him and to tell him that she loved him, but that was so like Sharif to avoid as much sentiment as possible. What he felt for her was something she knew in his care of her, which was what he was telling her to understand about Kadar. They really were so much alike, she thought to herself, quietly turning off the phone.

In the palace in Balahar, a third phone was replaced in its cradle, silently and unnoticed.

Chapter Ten

"I tell you that the marriage has not been consummated!" Queen Layla explained to her husband as he sat eating grapes from the fingers of a female concubine. Already Layla was put out by her husband's indolent pose, when he should have been in his office tending to his duties. "And furthermore, I now know exactly where Princess Serena is hiding."

"While I understand that you wish thanks for your diligence on my behalf," King Azzam said, not even glancing at his overexcited wife, "I can only repeat what I have said to you before—the fire of passion to reign over Balahar is long gone from me. I have a good life. I lack nothing. Why should I put my life and lifestyle at risk by angering King Zak?"

"Because it should be you," she insisted between clenched teeth. "*I* should be queen of both countries." Enraged by her husband's continued inattention, she snapped her fingers sharply to dismiss the concubine, who dropped the grapes and flew from the room on quiet, bare feet.

"Be careful, wife," Azzam stated none too gently. "I am not interested in one of your shrewish moods. You frightened that girl, and she is young and inexperienced at receiving the razor's edge of your tongue. I would not care to have her sweetness tempered by your cutting."

Layla sucked in her breath before lowering her eyes in a submissive gesture. It was only a gesture, however, as she fell to her knees in front of her husband, determined not to give in on the subject that concerned her most. "Forgive me, husband, but it pains me that you are not in your rightful position."

"I am where I want to be," he insisted, his tone impatient.

You could be even fatter and lazier with a hundred more concubines to feed you at the grander palace, she wanted to lash out, but wisely kept her words to herself. "As you wish, my husband. I only seek to do your will."

He got up from the velvet cushion where he'd lain, and Layla could feel his scorn radiate through the hairs on her lowered head.

"Then do my will and do not disturb me further with wild gossip and tales from the palace. We are as Allah has wished, and if you cannot live in this palace with me in peace rather than disharmony, I shall have you put out and your place taken by one who *will* please me.''

She raised her eyes only when she heard his footsteps in the hallway and knew his destination to be his room, where he would call back the young and lovely concubine to join with him.

Rage erupted inside Layla, not that her husband preferred his harem to her but that he was so insulated by the fruits of palace life that he had no wish to bestir himself to greatness. While she, *she* languished in a silk prison.

It was supposed to have been Rose who languished in a silk prison. Allah only knew that Layla had done her best to remove every vestige of Rose from her world. It ate at her bitterly that Rose was ever closer to securing the line of succession, while Layla was further away.

She wanted to scream.

But the loudness would bring servants, who would remark upon her manic state. A shriek would also further aggravate her husband, who was likely enjoying a quiet solitude in his room with the tender addition to the harem.

She clapped a hand over her mouth to keep her scream of frustration quiet—and remembered what the spy had heard Prince Sharif say to his sister. *Make your fourteen days count carefully. The time will pass swiftly, so be certain that you take advantage of this peace.*

If anyone knew how to destroy peace, it was she. If Prince Kadar wished tranquility for his princess in order to nurture their marriage, then her wedding present to him would be chaos.

No longer feeling the scream choke her, Princess Layla called in her adviser, Abdul-Rahim.

"Get *People* magazine on the phone, as well as any other American media that may be interested in a princess living on their soil disguised as a ordinary country cowgirl," she instructed.

"There are dozens of newspapers and magazines," the adviser told her. "As well as TV stations, no doubt."

"Then call them all," she rejoined. "After all, a princess should have all the attention her exalted position demands. Send any pictures and belongings of the princess we have in the palace if they wish them. And do it today. I want to see Serena celebrated around the world by tomorrow night."

And the marriage destroyed before it could blossom.

A blackhearted thought hit her with a pleasantly evil twist: Since Prince Kadar had married Serena in Balahar with Prince Makin's name, the marriage wasn't legal anyway—even if the two did utilize their "quiet" time to best purpose.

She smiled. In Balahar, consorting with a princess out of wedlock was an offense punishable by the strictest of measures—the most stringent, hanging;

the least, castration. In these modern times those measures possibly would not apply, but surely a prison term was a fitting place for a misguided prince who'd wandered into the royal fold by mistake…she'd be satisfied with a silk-lined prison for the son of King Ibrahim's beloved Rose.

"Abdul-Rahim," she called, regally rising to cross into the outer-office chamber. "Please make certain when you make the calls that the media realize the princess's marriage is a fake meant to fool the world, and most particularly the countries of Balahar and its neighbor, Sorajhee, which have direly prayed for a reason to believe this king has every subjects' best interests at heart." She shook her head, clucking her tongue. "Too bad for the country whose king is weak and unwilling to rule his people with the strength and leadership for which they pray."

SERENA COULD NOT bring herself to sneak into her husband's bed last night as Sharif had advised. She had needed time to think over what Sharif had told her, and had lain in her bed restless and tossing, considering every word he had said to her.

However, today was a new day, and she rose determined. If she wanted her prince, she was going to have to win him without negotiations, and without the alluring devices of the harem.

She would begin with the basics. The way to a

man's heart was through his stomach, according to an American talk show she'd listened to as she'd undressed last night. It was an odd way to get to a man's heart, and certainly no one in the palace would have thought to undertake the rite to passion that way, but she could do as the Americans while in America. Through his stomach it was.

That called for serving him breakfast in bed, and since Sharif instructed that Cade's bed was where she should be anyway, perhaps at least approaching his bedchamber would be the best way to start. This would be no small feat as she had always been the servee, and never the server. However, she did know what a breakfast tray should look like.

As a rule, her husband had said he started work early, not usually content to let overseers feed his famous horses. She slipped from her bed at three that morning to fix the meal.

After this attempt at pleasing him, she would put plan B into effect, to bring home the effect of plan A. Then plan C, which should combine nicely for a triple potion even her stalwart husband could not withstand.

CADE WAS AWAKENED by something moving in the dark in his bedroom. Whatever it was, it was none too stealthy—and it smelled horrible.

He flipped on the lamp beside his bed and startled

Serena so badly she nearly dropped the tray she carried.

"Serena! What are you doing?" He squinted at the alarm clock. "Especially at this hour of the morning?" He'd fantasized more than once in the past couple of days about her being in his bedroom—but this was not how he'd wanted her to come to his bed.

She smiled, nervously putting forth a tray for his inspection. He held back an urge to leap from the bed to open a window. "What is it, honey?"

"Your breakfast," she answered with a proud smile.

"How thoughtful of you." *This has to be a bad dream,* Cade thought. He sat up against the pillows she considerately fluffed up for him, and she arranged the tray over his lap. Eggs lay blackened at the edges, more than fried; bacon, which was underdone, curled like fatty snakes around the plate's edge. He held back an involuntary shudder.

"You are pleased?"

He smiled at the eagerness in her tone. "I am pleased. Thank you." Without hesitating further, he laid the tray on the floor beside the bed and jerked the tie of the apron that Serena wore. The apron slid to the floor. Then he pulled her into bed beside him and flipped off the bedside table lamp. The room fell to darkness and he sighed into his princess's hair as she lay spoon-style and stiff against him. "Relax,

Princess," he said softly. "Your gift has pleased me enormously. Now go to sleep."

Serena blinked with surprise in the dark, trying to gauge the success of her mission as Cade's breathing became regular behind her.

She'd gotten into his bed, as Sharif had suggested—and as she'd wanted. Her prince said he was pleased. Sharif's wistful voice came to her, speaking about his wish for a woman who knew how to quietly lay her head upon his chest and be content.

She hadn't planned for this, but Cade's strong arm tucked tightly around her waist as he lightly breathed into her hair felt more secure than anything she'd ever known in her life.

She relaxed, and just before she fell asleep, she thought that maybe she should bring her husband an early breakfast every day.

"YE GODS, WHAT WAS THAT?" Mac exclaimed, watching as his brother rinsed the plate containing Serena's breakfast preparations down the disposal.

"It was chiefly none of your business," Cade growled, "but since you are nosy, it was a consideration to me from Serena. She was trying to be thoughtful, and I'd appreciate any smart-aleck comments you may think to offer left unsaid."

Mac backed away from the sink warily. "No

problem. Just thought you'd decided to cook for yourself this morning, bro.''

Cade didn't reply to that. He *had* been touched by Serena's attempt to please him. If anyone had told him how much excitement a woman could bring into his life, he would have taken it as a negative statement. Women, he'd pretty much decided, took up as much time as training Arabians did.

Serena brought excitement rushing into his world, but he found himself liking it very much.

''What are you doing now?'' Mac asked, as Cade took down a skillet and picked up some eggs.

''Returning the favor to my princess.''

Mac shook his head. ''I think you've got it bad, bro.''

Cade didn't reply for a moment. ''I've actually got it better than I ever thought it could be,'' he said, quickly fixing up gently fried eggs, crispy hash browns and just-right bacon on a plate. He put that on the tray with a rose from the garden from the table. ''To be honest, I'm hoping it stays this good,'' he said as he left the room.

WHEN SERENA AWAKENED, Cade was gone and so was the breakfast tray. She was wearing the jeans she'd warn to cook breakfast, and decided maybe some of the silkier purchases from Victoria's Secret would be better for tomorrow's foray into Cade's bedroom. Her blouse was wrinkled from being slept in so she pulled it off, admiring the new brassiere Jessica had talked her into. She'd never seen anything quite like it, and she was positive neither had her husband.

She sat up, smiling at the thought.

The door opened suddenly, and she let out a tiny shriek as her husband entered the room, bearing a breakfast tray.

"Cade!" Forgetting all about her vow of a short, bravely silky nightgown and her exciting new brassiere intended for his viewing, she jerked the covers up to her chin.

He laughed at her instinctive modesty, and Serena felt herself blush.

"It's okay, Serena. I'm just returning the favor." He stood beside the bed, shaven and showered, his jeans fresh and his denim shirt pressed. Serena felt quite rumpled and unattractive. She wished she'd at least had a chance to comb her hair before her husband saw her! No woman with an eye to pleasing her husband allowed herself to be seen this way!

"Sit up, Serena," he commanded, but his tone was kind.

Shyly she sat up and lay against the pillows so that he could place the tray across her lap.

"It looks a lot different than what I cooked," she said, eyeing the food with interest. "I am unfamiliar with how this bacon meat should look, but Mac said you liked it."

"Mac?" Cade raised his brows at her.

"Oh, yes. He was in the kitchen when I went down at three o'clock. He said he was looking for a snack. But he did not help me with the preparation," she said. "He simply told me what you liked and then went back upstairs."

"He's a smart brother. You did a wonderful job with breakfast," Cade said, placing a quick kiss on the tip of her nose. "I wouldn't have wanted it any other way."

She quirked a brow at him. "But did you eat it?"

He grinned at her, and something inside her belly tightened. Her big husband made her slightly nervous, and yet she treasured him being so close to her.

"All gifts do not have to be used to be enjoyed," he said. "Have you ever heard that it's the thought that counts?"

"I do not remember." She wrinkled her forehead, but he smoothed her with gentle fingers.

"I very much appreciated the thought that you wanted to do something nice for me, Serena." He leaned close to her ear, and a light shiver passed over her. "And I very much enjoyed having my wife tucked up against me."

She looked up at him. "I enjoyed that, too."

"It's going to be difficult to keep separate bedrooms for two weeks if you're going to surprise me every morning."

Her eyelashes lowered. "I heard that it is good to keep a man guessing."

He sat down next to her on the bed, and Serena knew that there was no way she could eat her breakfast with Cade watching her. "I do not like guessing. If you're going to sneak into my bedroom at three-thirty on a consistent basis, I'll have to set a booby trap for you."

"I do not sneak!" She raised her eyes to stare at him. "I knocked, but you did not answer."

"At that hour, no." He gave her a wry grin. "So maybe it would be less trouble if I just kept you in my room. That way I could anchor you to the bed when you decided to make my breakfast. You don't have to do that for me, Serena."

"I know you think that princesses do not cook, Cade, but if your mother does, then so can I." She leaned forward earnestly, and the sheet drooped slightly.

"Where is your shirt?" he asked, his eyes suddenly serious and direct on the light blue bra strap.

She pulled the sheet back up. "I was about to change when you walked in," she said as airily as she could, though she was becoming nervous all over again.

He was silent as he considered her. Serena sat still, trying to judge the new look she had never seen in his eyes before. Then he reached out and with one finger, gently drew the sheet down to expose her entire bosom.

"You purchased unusual brassieres, I see," he said huskily.

"You said you wanted me wearing them, and this is what Jessica suggested," she said earnestly. "It has a magical button here, you see, which is, the saleslady claimed, 'unlike any other bra made in the world!' If you do this," she said, touching the button once, "it does *this,* and tightens the cleavage. And you can do this three times—" she went click, click on the button again "—for a look no man can fail to appreciate, or so the saleslady made me believe."

She met his gaze hopefully. Cade hadn't moved, hadn't so much as blinked.

She didn't think that was a very good sign. "It's called a Click bra," she said uncertainly. "If you do not like it, I will take it back at once and tell the saleslady not to trick the Princess of Balahar again."

He let out a long, low exhalation of breath as he got up from the table. He shoved his hands into his jeans pockets as he stared first into her eyes, then back at the magical bra the saleslady had hawked with such blandishments. "Eat your breakfast," was all he said as he finally left the room.

Serena lowered her head. Neither breakfast in bed nor her miraculous bra seemed to have had much impact. Cade was determined to treat her like a forbidden princess he'd married without fully considering his actions.

Suddenly his head poked back inside the room. She jumped, nearly upsetting her tray.

"Serena, keep the bra," he said before quickly retreating.

She smiled as the door closed. Maybe her husband wasn't as immune as he tried so hard to appear!

Good cooking, dress for success, and what was the third idea she'd gotten from the American talk show?

"Oh, yes. Show interest in his work," she said, snapping her fingers.

That was plan C, which would surely show Prince Kadar how well she could fit into his world!

Chapter Eleven

An hour later, Cade went to the barn, his mind torn. He'd run a quick errand, chafing because he'd just left the most desirable woman he'd ever seen up in his bed—his mind was definitely back there. In all her innocence, Serena could have no idea of the wallop she packed as she offered her beauty to him without guile—clad in lingerie he'd wanted to pull from her body *immediately*.

When her cleavage, as she'd called it, rounded up over the light blue fabric to make plump half-moons, all he could think of was that she looked like a white-skin peach he desperately wanted to bite into.

But no lingerie was going to cause him to lose his self-control. He had eleven more days with Serena before she had to make up her mind to return home. Hopefully that was long enough for her to decide whether she liked him, liked his family, liked Texas. He reminded himself that she was innocent;

she had no full concept of the temptation she lay before him.

Gritting his teeth, he told himself he could hold out.

"Not that I counted on Jessica to launch the Victoria's Secret war on me," he grumbled to himself as he went to grab a pitchfork in the barn.

"Trouble?" Mac asked.

He stopped, turning to look at his brother. "Oh, hey, Mac. I didn't see you."

"And a good day it is, too," Mac said cheerfully. "For most people, anyway. Something thorny under your saddle, bro?"

"There is nothing under my saddle," Cade said tightly. "With Mother and Jessica firmly aligned against me, I don't need you encouraging Serena to bring me my favorite breakfast, and whatever else."

Mac laughed. "She asked what you liked. I told her."

"Yes, she mentioned that."

"What did it hurt, Cade? I like Serena. I'm not going to ignore her just because you do."

"What the hell is that supposed to mean?" Cade demanded.

Mac leaned against a post and grinned at his brother. "If you ignore a woman, other men are going to pay attention to her."

"You had your chance at her. As I recall, you passed."

His brother laughed at him. "You sound jealous. Kind of eaten up with it."

Cade glowered. "I have no comment to make to encourage your idiocy. If you are trying to make me jealous, it won't work."

Mac turned back to what he was doing. "Okay."

The easy acquiescence displeased Cade. "Is that what you're trying to do?"

Mac shrugged, his shoulder muscles straining against the blue work shirt as he lifted a saddle. "You said it wouldn't matter, so why do you care? Since you *don't* care, that is."

"I care," Cade said on a growl.

"Well, okay, then. Shut the hell up and quit acting like Mr. Coldhearted." Mac turned back around to face him. "All I meant was that Serena needs a friend, Cade. I like her. We get along real well, mainly because she reminds me a lot of Jessica and I'm comfortable with that kind of gal. And I see Serena knocking herself out to please her husband, and I think with a little aim in the right direction, maybe my dense brother will finally wake up and appreciate what she's trying to do for him."

Cade was silent.

"It's what I'd do for anybody who was a guest at the ranch. Making Serena comfortable is the least I can do for the poor, stranded girl."

"She's not stranded. I check on her all the time."

"Yeah, like a great hulking warden checking in

on his prisoner. Or maybe,'' Mac said slowly, ''more like a little kid keeps checking his cage to make sure the pretty bird he's caught hasn't flown away.''

Cade pressed his lips together as he stared at his brother. ''I get your point,'' he finally said. ''Exactly what is your advice to me on the matter of Serena, Mac? Go ahead, spit it out, don't pull your punches,'' he said with some sarcasm.

''If you want her to be happy here—and that's supposedly the reason for your, um, separation from her—you need to romance her. Not the other way around. Or at least don't let her efforts go unreciprocated.''

''It's not that easy,'' Cade said quietly. ''She's a hard woman to be around.''

Mac cocked a brow at him. ''Oh?''

Cade thought about the clicking bra and the soft, peachy-white skin. He thought about how she felt up against him in the night. ''Maybe I do avoid her a little, but it isn't my intention for her to feel unwanted.''

''Oh, you're trying to be heroic,'' Mac said with a dawning tone. ''Maybe you should tell her that when you're around her, you feel like you're about to pop your zipper.''

''For crying out loud!'' Cade stared at his brother. ''I can't tell her that!''

''Why not? A woman who's worked as hard as

she has for your attention would probably be happy to hear it.''

''Well, I can't, that's all. I can't say something like that to a princess! And besides which,'' he said quietly, darting a look around him, ''you don't know Serena. If she knew how close she is to getting what she wants, she'll unleash all the temptations of Eve on me, and I'm only so much man. I can't stay away from her forever!'' He paced to the opposite end of the barn and then back. ''I can hang on until she knows her mind. I can be that much of a gentleman.''

Mac laughed. ''We're not going to see you for a week once you finally let your guard down, bro.''

Cade shook his head. ''Two weeks, I hope. Hey, listen, I'll be back in ten to help you with this, okay?''

''Where are you going?''

''There's something I forgot to tell Serena,'' he called over his shoulder. Maybe he'd better tell her how much he liked her, he thought as he strode off. Maybe just telling her not to return the bra and fixing her a reciprocal breakfast wasn't enough for a woman. If Mac was right, she just might get tired of being at The Desert Rose.

And that was the exact opposite of what he'd been trying to do. He still wouldn't make love with her—he didn't want to rush her.

But he could certainly do more to let her know that he enjoyed having her around.

"THERE, NOW," Mac said to Serena as she came out from behind the stall door where she'd been currying a horse in her effort to be a part of Cade's life. "Feel better?"

Serena blinked. "I had no idea he felt that way! It seems like an elaborate scheme to keep me, Mac. I would never have thought that Cade would believe that staying away from me would make me want to stay."

He laughed. "I don't think he'd thought his plan all the way through. Everything's happened pretty fast. Besides which, you've yanked a pretty good knot in my brother. I've never seen him act like this about a woman before."

A warm glow of hope filled Serena. "You haven't?"

"Nope. He looked like he was about to bite my head off when I pricked his jealousy a little bit."

She smiled. "He did not sound too happy."

"No. He did not."

"So now what do I do?"

"Can I make a suggestion, Serena?"

"You know him much better than I do. I will be glad to hear anything you have to say."

"You don't want to go back to Balahar, do you?"

Serena lowered her gaze for a moment. "I do, one

day. I want to see my family and my home. But if you are asking if I could be happy here, the answer is yes. I consider my place to be at Cade's side.''

''Well, then, let's have you be a bit more elusive.''

''Elusive?''

Mac nodded, grinning. ''We've got him feeling guilty now. A couple of days where you don't seem all that consumed to please him wouldn't hurt the old princely ego much.''

Serena considered that, thinking that plans A, B and C hadn't been exactly foolproof. ''But I do not like to appear aloof to my prince,'' she said. ''It is not done that way in my country. Our women in the harem show their eagerness so that they will be chosen. Otherwise, how will the prince know that they are willing?''

''Sometimes, when one is setting out bait, it's best to let the prey get close to check it out, whet its appetite. Then the prey will follow it right into the trap, or onto the hook, if that sounds less mercenary.''

She frowned. ''My husband is not something to be caught like a fish.''

''Well, you've tried it the woman's way. I'm just telling you the man's way. We're hunters at heart, basically. The thrill of pursuit doesn't scare us off. Or at least it won't in my brother's case, let me say that. Me, I'm a much different kind of guy," he said quickly. "This plan wouldn't work on me."

"You're just saying that in case you ever bring home a woman. You don't want me telling her this."

Mac winked at her. "It strikes me that you're a very smart woman, Serena, and yes, my words could very much come back to haunt me someday."

They laughed with each other for a moment. "Do you have a lady you like?" Serena asked softly.

He shook his head a bit reluctantly. "I...met one that I liked once."

"Where is she?"

"I don't know. Believe it or not, I don't even know her name."

"Oh. That is sad!" Serena said. She leaned close to give him a fast hug, hoping to erase the hopelessness in his eyes.

"Serena!" Cade roared. "I've been looking all over for you!"

Her breath jumped into her throat, tightening it, and instinctively she would have leaped away from Mac for fear of her actions being misunderstood. But Mac's hand pressed her back, stilling her, and Serena remembered his words.

"You found me, husband," she said archly, rather than offering the dire and fearful apology that would have been due in her country. "Is there something you wanted?"

''I want to talk to you.'' He strode forward to where she stood, her hand still on Mac's shoulder, patting nervously, before she went to retrieve the currycomb she'd left in the stall.

''I am listening, my husband,'' she said, not meanly, but not eager as she had been in the past.

He hesitated, uncertain.

No doubt wondering why I am not jumping to please him, Serena thought with a secret smile.

''It…it worried me when I could not find you,'' Cade finally offered. ''I wanted to check on you.''

Serena glanced at him as she led the horse out to walk it down to the enclosure for hosing down. ''As you can see, I am fine. Although I thank you for your concern.''

He frowned as she met his gaze with a heart-tugging smile. ''You're not hanging out with Jessica today?''

''She went into town, and your mother is busy with a project, so I decided it was time to get outdoors and learn about your ranch,'' she said airily.

''I'll give you a tour—''

She shook her head. ''It won't be necessary. But thank you.'' Turning the water on, she began rinsing down the horse's back, and then the front legs.

Cade turned to stare at his brother. ''I'm trying.''

Mac nodded. ''You are.''

''She doesn't seem all that deprived of my attention,'' Cade said thoughtfully. He wondered at the change in Serena's attitude. Usually she was delighted to have him near her.

"Well," Mac said, his grin huge as he turned back to what he'd been doing before the two lovebirds had flown into the barn, "with all your experience with women, Cade, you'll be able to figure this out soon enough."

Cade glanced at his brother suspiciously, wondering if the cough he heard was Mac's attempt to swallow a laugh. His gaze returned to Serena, but she blithely ignored him.

All his experience with women wasn't helping him with Serena, and Mac darn well knew it.

Even Cade knew it, and he didn't like it one bit.

"I don't like women who change from minute to minute," he groused.

"Did you say something, my prince?" Serena called, her smile just as inviting as it had ever been for him.

His heart dropped into his stomach as he stared at her. Even damp and slightly grubby, she was intoxicating. "I said I wish you wouldn't work like this," he fibbed. He warmed to his subject. "You're a princess. I don't want you doing hard work."

"I am a princess," she agreed. "And I shall do as I like."

That was new. She had never said anything like that to him before. Cade warily approached his bride. "I would be embarrassed if your father knew about you doing this type of thing. He would think I had no intention of treating you as you deserve.''

She threw him a wry glance. ''Do you think me incapable of using my mouth to tell my father that this is my choice? To bathe horses rather than sit in the house like a useless piece of furniture?''

''Maybe I should take you into town,'' Cade said helplessly, caught between wanting to romance her and wanting her to stop working. ''I'm sure you didn't do this kind of thing in Balahar.''

She smiled at him. ''I would not have been allowed.''

''Then you shouldn't be allowed here! Let me take you into town. We can eat lunch out—''

''My husband,'' she interrupted with determination. ''Please be quiet. Your worrying is giving me a headache.''

''Wow! Is that the princess?'' someone's triumphant voice suddenly exclaimed. ''She looks just like her picture!'' Lights flashed inside the dim barn. A horse reared, startled by the commotion of six strange men crowding around Cade and Serena. One shook Cade's hand, holding out a press card. ''We're from—''

But Cade didn't hear the rest. All he could see was Serena, wet and bedraggled, shrinking up against the big horse in an attempt to shield herself from the photographers' assault.

"Out!" he shouted. "Every last one of you—get out!"

THE PICTURES ON the evening news that night were no consolation to Cade. Serena looked frightened out of her wits, like a waif who had been caught in a barn.

He burned, knowing that the pictures would make their way to Balahar, and to the king's eye.

"I can't understand how they found out Serena was here," Rose said. "Now that they know, your chance at privacy is gone, Cade."

So much for them getting to know each other without a thousand eyeballs prying into their business. Cade groaned. "I just hate to think what her father is going to believe when he sees those pictures."

"He is not going to be happy," Rose confirmed. "You should be prepared for anything to happen."

"What are you saying?" Mac asked. "That they may send a plane for Serena and drag her back home?"

"More likely a delegation will be sent at once to check on her. I can't believe that King Zak will simply take Serena's word on the phone that she is happy here. But perhaps he will. They seem close to each other."

"It was probably only a matter of time before the press learned about Serena," Vi said, who had come, with her husband, to discuss the disaster that had befallen the ranch.

"I hate to bring this up," Randy said, "but it isn't going to be easy on the hands to work with strangers trooping around all the time. They won't mean to, but they'll drop trash and tear up the dirt paths where they park their cars and trucks."

"So it's just going to get worse." Cade tried to imagine the scope of what was about to happen to The Desert Rose.

"Well, it's one thing for them to believe that the princess is just here visiting," Vi said. "But they might start digging, and if it gets out that you two are married under unusual circumstances, I don't think you'll ever see an end to the photographers camped outside."

"Which brings us to the problem of the princes' and princess's lives being jeopardized. We can't possibly provide security with people coming and going all the time. Posting No Trespassing signs will help, but the more intrepid photographers will ignore them. And let's not forget about zoom lens cameras," Randy reminded them. "This will be very difficult on our fifteen boarders, not to mention the horses."

The phone rang, making them all groan.

"That will be the king," Cade said. His gaze met Serena's.

"I will talk to my father and explain," she said quietly. "After all, this is my fault."

"King Zak, on the phone for Serena," Jessica called cheerfully.

Cade watched as Serena got to her feet and crossed into the study, closing the door behind her. "Can we ask for some police protection? I really don't like to think about Serena being followed by strangers all the time. She needs a bodyguard."

"You make a very good point, Cade. She needs you," Rose said, rising. "You guard her for the rest of her stay in Bridle. Don't let her out of your sight. I want you to stick to her like wet jeans. If she decides to stay here and marry you under your real name, properly, we'll deal with that at that time. For now, she is your greatest responsibility."

Cade's jaw dropped, his protest immediate and yet left unspoken by the purposeful glint in his mother's eyes as she passed him. After a moment, Vi and Randy followed her into the kitchen. Then Jessica left as well.

Deserters, every last one of them, to dump the princess on him. He couldn't spend every minute of every day with her. He couldn't be around her that much! She'd tease him, torture him, tempt him—

He caught his brother's smirk, wide and annoying, as if Mac knew exactly what Cade was thinking.

"You take good care of the princess," Mac said, laughing as he left the room.

Cade pressed his lips together. Once upon a time, he'd felt powerful, invincible. He'd known who he was, and felt in control of his world. Totally confident and in command. He was a man who hopped into his jet and flew to foreign countries to make deals; he was impressive and respected. No one would have dared to toy with him.

All that had changed with the arrival of a certain lady in his life—and now he had to figure out how to get it all back together again. Soon. Because sticking to Serena like wet jeans was going to be the hardest thing he'd ever done. He was pretty certain he wasn't capable of being her bodyguard. Protecting her from others was one thing.

Protecting her from himself had already proved painfully challenging.

Chapter Twelve

"Mom," Jessica said as they grouped together in the kitchen. "I had a friend call me tonight, and I was wondering if you would mind an extra person staying at the ranch. I know it's probably not such a great idea right now, but I was hoping she could help me with ranch paperwork and a few other jobs."

Randy kissed his wife briefly on the forehead. "I'll go warn Jan and Mickey and the gang about the onslaught we're bracing for. You folks excuse me." He left the kitchen, and Vi's eyes followed him for a moment before she returned her attention to Jessica.

"I don't mind," she said. "Although you might warn her about the extra excitement we may be having."

"Abbie is looking for a change," Jessica said with a smile. "I'll tell her that the photographers are here taking pictures of the horses before an upcoming show. That way the royalty thing won't come up, Aunt Rose.''

''I worry that it won't stay hidden much longer.'' Vi got up to look out the window.

Jessica's gaze followed hers, where Randy stood talking to Savannah, a boarder at The Desert Rose. *Warning her about the possible invasion,* Jessica thought, and wondered why her mother suddenly looked so sad.

Ella brought in the mail, thumping it down on the table with less than her customary cheer. ''I'm not going to be able to take a breath without worrying that one of those photographers is going to ask me something,'' she complained. ''They even looked over my shoulder to see what I pulled out of the mailbox!''

Rose shook her head. ''I cannot imagine how they got wind of the princess being here.'' She reached out, her fingers instantly grasping the envelope with the king's royal seal on it. ''I think King Zak has made good on his promise and sent the wedding pictures,'' she said eagerly, tearing open the envelope.

Jessica, Ella and Vi all peered over her shoulder. ''Pretty fancy for a quick wedding,'' Jessica observed. ''Doesn't Cade look handsome? Like a real Arabian prince! I mean, he is real,'' she said hastily. ''It's just hard to think of him that way when he's around The Desert Rose.''

But it wasn't her son, Prince Kadar, who had Rose's attention. She stared at the four people in the photograph: the king, Serena, Kadar beside her, and then Prince Sharif beside him.

All the world seemed to drop away from Rose as she gazed at the prince she'd never seen.

''Hey, kinda funny how Cade and that Sharif guy look just like each other,'' Jessica said.

''Like peas in a pod,'' Ella commented, going off to put some mail upstairs in Cade's office.

''They could pass for brothers rather than brothers-in-law,'' Vi stated.

Rose's blood ran cold. She'd thought the same thing.

Prince Sharif and Serena were related by adoption. King Zak had adopted Serena when his best friend, her father, had died. But Sharif had come to him at birth, unlike Serena. Rose counted back the years to her final pregnancy. The baby had been taken from her at birth, a reality that had broken her heart and further assured her descent into depression. She'd even been told there had never been a pregnancy, never been a child. Yet despite the times she began to doubt herself, she knew deep in her heart that she had given birth to her beloved Ibrahim's fourth child.

She glanced back at the picture again. Sharif and Kadar stared into the camera—dark skinned, confident, astonishingly handsome. Pure prince. Both with Ibrahim's features spread between them, unless her wistful mind was playing tricks on her.

Surely Layla's treachery hadn't run that far?

SERENA STRODE OUT of the office after her phone conversation with her father. He had been upset, and that she could understand. He had very nearly commanded her to come home at once.

That she was not willing to do. She soothed his king's pride and explained that she had been tending the horses because she had wanted to—not because her husband had allowed it.

She assured him that she was safe at The Desert Rose. And then she decided that, since she currently was the press's only target, she would tell them everything they thought they wanted to know.

It wasn't all that newsworthy. Or, at least, the story she intended to tell them wouldn't be. Tucking her wedding rings into her jeans pocket, she marched down to the side of the road where the six reporters were parked. With a winning smile, she perched on top of the fence, hooking her boots around the lower rail as she'd seen Jan and Mickey and the other ranch hands do.

The reporters snapped to attention, their cameras clicking rapidly.

"So," Serena said, "what do you want to know?"

"What are you doing in a little town in Texas?" one called.

"I'm on vacation. Haven't you heard of dude ranches? Princesses need to get away, too," she said smartly.

"That's it?" someone called. "What made you pick The Desert Rose?"

She shrugged. "I heard there was peace and quiet here."

They laughed, a bit embarrassed.

"What do you like to eat, Princess?"

"Oh, come on, now. You can do better than that," she teased. "What do you eat? Everybody in Texas eats a lot of meat and potatoes, and as much Mexican food as they possibly can, right?"

The reporters stared at her, their questions stilled.

"What? That's all?" she coaxed.

"We just thought there'd be more," one explained.

She shook her head. "It's not all that exciting to be a princess."

"You got your eye on a prince?" a female reporter asked.

Serena blinked. "Hmm. My father will arrange a marriage for me," she said primly. It was the truth. He had. The arrangement had gone awry since she'd married the incorrect brother, but that wasn't a detail she was interested in sharing.

"Will you mind having an arranged marriage?" the female reporter pressed.

I won't if you go away so we can get on with our marriage, Serena thought, but she smiled good-naturedly. "It is our custom." After a moment, she slid off the fence. "I'd like to get back to washing my horse. He spooks easy, so it's best if you folks don't pop in on him like that anymore. He might jump and injure himself or me."

The reporters shifted uncomfortably.

"Sure, Princess," someone said.

And that was the end of her first press conference. Or so she thought, until she felt Cade take hold of her arm.

The cameras began whirring all over again.

CADE WASN'T CERTAIN he'd be able to play the role of bodyguard. He was considering the sexual angle of the matter. Proximity to his wife meant wanting her, and that was all there was to that. He was hanging on heroically by a thread not to ravish a woman who either went braless, wore clicking bras that enticed or merry widows that made his breath stop in his chest.

He was not a very merry husband. She was determined to seduce him, and he was determined that she see exactly what she was getting into with him. Right now, she could still change her mind; she could return home and procure an annulment. He owed her that, at least.

But then, as he stood pondering these thoughts, trying to corral his last vestiges of good sense into his moral obligation to be her bodyguard, he saw his little wife sashaying down the road to the reporters' command post.

He'd followed quickly, cursing under his breath. Bodyguarding her was going to be as easy as holding on to a rainbow.

He didn't get there in time to hear what she'd said to the press, but he took hold of her arm to lead her off. He would tell her in the future she should not leave the house without consulting him. They did not know these reporters, and they did not owe them any information.

Serena snapped her arm out of his grasp.

"Princess—" he said, but she cut him off.

"I am fine on my own, please," she stated.

"Hey," one of the reporters called, "how 'bout him, Princess? He might suit you."

Someone else said, the voice teasing, "Hey, how about me, Princess?"

Cade's temper flew clean out of his head as he turned. "The princess is spoken for. There will be no further press conferences. She has said all she will be saying. We would appreciate it if you remove yourselves from the premises at once."

Angered by Cade's words, though they'd been

soothed by Serena's time with them, someone said, "Hey, the princess was just being nice to us, which is more than I can say for you."

Cade began to speak, but Serena jerked forward, dragging him with her since he had her by the arm.

"Just be quiet," she said under her breath. "You're making everything worse!"

Cade was so startled by his normally submissive wife's sharp words to him that he could only allow her to pull him off into the barn. Once inside, they faced each other, hands on hips.

"I had it under control," she said.

"I am your protector," he stated unequivocally.

"I did not need your protection then, and I will not be needing it at all."

"My mother has decided that, for the duration of your visit, I am to be your bodyguard."

"The duration…" Serena's face went paler than normal. "What does that mean?"

Cade halted, realizing that in his anger his words had come out quite different from how he'd intended them. "I mean that I am to take care of you while you are here, which I've been trying to do all along, as a matter of fact, except you won't stay put!" He had a thing or two to tell her, and it was past time he said it. Seeing her little bottom encased in tight jeans strolling off toward a den of men had displeased him mightily—he was damn sure he was within his princely rights to be extremely upset with his wife. "You would not have approached any men, known or otherwise, in your country in the manner in which you did a moment ago, am I correct?"

Serena lowered her eyes. "I would not."

"What would have happened if you had?"

"It is not done in my country," she admitted. "I do not know. I suppose I would have been punished."

"Married or otherwise, you would not go off with a band of strange men?"

"No. I would not," she admitted.

"Then I certainly expect the same while you are here!"

That brought her head up. "I do not like the way you make it sound as if I won't be here long! I did what I thought was best! I am sorry if you are offended, but it was important to me that your family not be bothered because of me. If that angers you, then I am sorry."

Cade crossed his arms, trying to remain angry, but he could not. He put his arms down and pulled her against his chest instead. "You frightened me," he said gruffly. "I was already feeling out of my league because being your protector is going to be difficult."

"A big strong man like you should be able to keep up with little tiny me with one hand tied behind his back," Serena mumbled against his chest.

He drew her auburn hair through his fingers. Her slender body melted up against his made him think about things he figured he shouldn't be thinking just yet, since he didn't want to rush the princess. "Yes, but we just established that you were protecting *me*. And my family."

"I do not want to be an inconvenience for you," she murmured. "You are always talking about how much I will have to adjust to life in Texas. It seems to me that you are the one having to do all the adjusting with a princess on your ranch. By spinning my tale for the reporters, I merely thought to ease the situation."

He tipped her head back so that he could stare down into her light emerald eyes. "You used to finish a sentence like that with 'my prince,' or some other respectful title."

She blinked. "I am not addressing you in such a manner anymore, in case you mistake the terms of respect for my subservience."

"Subservience!" Cade exclaimed. "You may be the least subservient woman I have ever known, besides Jessica. No man's going to marry her, because she's too bossy. Too stubborn. Don't you dare be like her."

Serena smiled as Cade tugged on her hair for emphasis as she continued looking up at him. "Prince Makin seems to think it would be best if I treated you with less deference. He wondered if perhaps it had all gone to your head.''

Cade groaned. "Excuse me, but Prince Makin is not exactly an expert in the love-life department. He has none, so I wouldn't go on his advice."

"He likes somebody," Serena said. "Or maybe he liked somebody. But when he talks about her, he seems a little sad."

"Nope," Cade said decisively. "He had a bad breakup once, but he's over that now. He hasn't had a girlfriend since then, hasn't wanted one. Which is how I came to be on the plane to Balahar."

"You were checking out the goods," Serena accused. "You never intended to stand in for your brother."

"I may not have been then," Cade said, his gaze firmly caught by Serena's full, lightly peach lips, "but you are not to take advice or anything else from Prince Makin. He may be my twin, but we are as different as night and day. Is that clear, Princess?"

"It is clear," she said breathlessly.

He lowered his lips to hers, kissing her the way he'd wanted to ever since she'd come into his life. Her lips parted beneath his, and somehow the kiss went deeper than he'd intended. He couldn't stop kissing her. He wanted more than he would allow himself, and with a groan, he pulled himself away from her.

Serena looked at him with pleasure. "Although you should know that Prince Makin says that allowing you to taste the bait is the best way to hook you," she said without guile, while she smiled teasingly at him. "Or maybe it was the best way to entice you into my trap. It had something to do with men enjoying the pursuit, I am positive."

"He said that, did he? Doctor Lovelorn thinks he's got all the answers?" Cade shook his head. "And to think that wonderful advice comes from all his experience with women."

She tilted her head up so that her lips pouted invitingly. Her hands reached out to lightly touch his shirtfront. Cade knew exactly what she was doing, his little minx of a wife. "I'm not going to kiss you," he said. "I'm not going to validate such silly advice. I'm not about to—"

On her tiptoes, Serena pressed her lips against Cade's. He felt sheer desire pour through him as her breasts brushed his chest.

"Kiss me," she whispered, "my prince. My sheikh. My bodyguard."

He did, hungrily, realizing only after the kiss was finished that she had reverted to form with her respectful address of him.

And he had given in to her, like a haystack collapsing in a winter storm.

"Prince Makin doesn't know everything," he muttered, as they drew apart. "You get those wedding rings out of your pocket, put them back on, and don't let me see them off you again. I should spank you.''

Serena laughed at him, a low, satisfied chuckle that was all woman and had shivers of anticipation running up his spine. ''I think you will be my true husband very soon,'' she said.

She turned and left the barn. Cade rubbed his lips ruefully. He could still taste her, could still feel her silky-soft hair on his fingertips.

''I'm only so much man,'' he grumbled. ''I'm not superhuman.'' His mother had assigned him to be bodyguard; his brother was dispensing advice. Jessica had tossed the Victoria's Secret bag of allure into the arsenal his wife was using against him.

There was nothing he wanted to do more than bury himself inside his teasing temptation of a wife. She wanted him, and that was highly seductive.

He wanted her, so much so that he felt burning with feverish desire.

Consummation meant irrevocable marriage with Serena. Did she expect him to want the throne? He did not. Reporters coming here today had scared him to death. The last thing he wanted was to raise a family in a glaring spotlight. He didn't want any of his children to be in a royal succession. He raised horses for a living, and that was all he ever intended to do. His family lived quietly, anonymous solitude all they wanted. Today Serena tried to insure that solitude by spinning an uninteresting yarn for the reporters.

He begrudgingly admired that, except that he was supposed to be protecting her.

She had been pursuing him, but now Mac had told her that she should allow him to pursue her.

She was his wife, but she was her own woman. A frown knotted his brow. With Serena, it was as if he lived in a maze from which he could not escape. Just as soon as he thought he'd figured out one angle of her, she threw another angle his way.

He was fairly positive he didn't have control of his situation, nor his wife.

"I will not fall for these tricks," he assured himself, "even though she's been up-front about all of it, it might encourage her to become more devious. I'll simply tell her I will never be interested in being in the line of succession, and if she wants to stay here with me, then she'll just have to forget that she was ever a princess."

And then maybe they could get down to the business of being just a man, just a woman who were brought together by an arranged marriage.

It was a nice and easy equation, but he had a funny feeling it wouldn't be as simple to fit Serena into it. He had an itch for that little gal—and she was having too much fun providing the source!

LAYLA READ the evening papers with displeasure. "It says nothing here about the secret royal family living in the States, or Serena's unconsummated and dishonorable marriage to the wrong prince. She's a tricky little devil, I'll have to credit her for that.''

Azzam ignored her as he read the sports section. He was far more interested in the hockey finals being played in the States. All that bruising, crushing excitement in the end of May! For summer, there was also American baseball, and the French Open tennis games in France. He wished he was still fit enough for a game of convivial tennis.

''Azzam, do you hear me?''

He did, but he wouldn't encourage her. He'd tried to tell Layla more than once that he wasn't interested in wresting rule from anyone. For that matter, Azzam wasn't interested in anything his wife had to say. He despised her scheming nature. Perhaps it was true what he'd read in a book he'd gotten from the States once, that behind every good man there was a good woman. Layla was not a good wife to him, a benefit the first wife should be. He had not accorded her a place of enjoyment in his heart since he learned the truth of his brother Ibrahim's death. He far preferred the harem, and the young girls there who made him feel as if perhaps he could still play tennis and—in his wildest fantasies—hard-hitting hockey on an ice-cold rink.

He went back to daydreaming about body-challenging sports.

Layla slipped from the room to order her adviser to put in another tip to the American press, although they hadn't done what she hoped for the first time. Maybe international press calls were needed to flush the imposter couple out of their honeymoon hideout.

Amazed by what she hadn't thought of before, Layla stood rooted in place. International press. Of course.

The least it would do was break up a fake marriage, which was dangerous to her rightful throne.

More than that, the press *would* flush a royal family out of hiding. Rose and her sons were cowards. If their deed had not been wrong, they would have done it in the light of day instead of skulking off without a royal wedding. King Zak should be exposed for the fraud he had put over on the people of Balahar.

Azzam deserved the place due him as Ibrahim's brother, Layla thought bitterly. *But now Rose is marrying her sons into the Balahar family by some sleight of hand, some trick of smoke. She intends to seize power and regain what she always wanted most—to cheat me out of my crown. She wants to be ruling queen of a combined kingdom of Balahar and Sorajhee. I will be reduced to a minor figurehead with mere dress-up duties.*

She stole my betrothed.

She will not steal my crown.

Chapter Thirteen

"Okay, here's the deal," Cade told Serena imperiously when he found her—where else?—in the barn. "I've been thinking about this, ever since you effectively rid us of the reporters. The princess thing is a lot of trouble. I wanted to treat you like one, but you were determined to be a plain ol' American girl so you could share my life. The hassle with the press changed my mind. You can be a plain ol' American girl, but I don't want to hear any complaints when your velvet cushion isn't plumped up for you regularly."

Serena hung up the halter she carried and stared at her husband with a smile. "I told you that when in Texas, it is best to do as the Texans do. You came to Balahar and acted like a prince. Maybe you will do so again. It is only fitting that I am like an American woman here."

"And that's another thing we need to straighten out," he said. "If we don't have any princesses on this ranch, we sure don't have any princes. I'm never going back to Balahar to be a prince.''

"But surely to visit?" Serena asked, thinking her husband did not realize exactly what he was asking of her.

"Well, maybe," he conceded. "Sometimes."

She kissed him on the cheek. "You are a good man. Now please give me the keys to your truck."

He recoiled, startled. She grinned, reaching into his pocket to hook the keys out with a finger. "All American girls need to know how to drive, and American girls who live on a ranch need especially to be able to drive a truck."

"Not my truck!"

"Most particularly your truck," Serena said, enjoying the expression on her husband's face. "Why does that scare you?"

"It doesn't scare me because it's not going to happen. No one drives my truck but me."

Serena laughed. "Teach me, husband. Otherwise someone else will have to teach me, and we will miss a prime opportunity to get to know each other as man and wife. The idea of teaching me should appeal to you."

Cade glowered. "I'm trying to figure out how I always seem to get caught in your net of words. Just as soon as I'm positive I'm not going to do something, you change my mind somehow."

She jingled his keys at him. "I want to learn to

be an independent woman, and no woman is truly independent unless she has her own transportation. We are too far from buses and subways, and I do not wish to be stranded in a foreign country—''

''I do not wish to have my gears ground into powder and my transmission dumped into the dirt!''

She raised her brows at him. ''Surely you are a better teacher than that!''

''Serena,'' he said on a growl, ''that is not what I meant at all, and you darn well know it.''

''Oh, then you are suggesting I am too stupid to learn!'' she exclaimed. She backed toward his shiny truck, jingling his keys at him again teasingly. ''I am sorry to be so ignorant that my husband cannot even teach me how to drive.''

Cade ran to catch her as she opened the driver's door and leaped into the seat, locking the door behind her. He darted around to the passenger door and got in, glaring at her.

''Why do you think that in American movies so many people make love in their vehicles?'' she asked.

''Okay, that's *it*,'' he stated. ''No one teaches you to drive except me.''

She beamed. ''You are so generous, husband.''

''No, I'm not. I…I…you shouldn't think about things like that,'' he said, his tone stern.

''Not think about making love?'' Serena raised her eyebrows. ''I'm married, am I not? I want to be a proper wife. I might like making love in your truck,'' she said, ''although I can't quite envision how two people can manage such a feat.''

''Serena,'' Cade said from between gritted teeth. ''Here is the ignition. Put the key in here, and turn it until the engine comes to life.''

He ran his sleeve across his forehead. She grinned.

''Now, I put this key into this opening—oh, see how well it fits—and then I turn it on, and the engine roars to life!'' She gave him a triumphant smile. ''I like driving, Cade.''

He groaned. ''Don't break your arm patting yourself on the back, Princess. Now, see this behind the steering wheel? This is the shift.''

Glancing at her to see if she was paying attention, Cade halted. ''You are listening?''

''To every word,'' Serena answered, her eyes on his firm lips. ''You have pointed out the shift.''

''Good. Now shift it into Reverse, and back up until you get to the grassier part of the driveway. It will be easier for you to turn around rather than drive backward the length of the driveway.''

''Oh, I should think so.'' Serena moved the truck into reverse and like silk, it moved ever so slightly backward.

''Press on the gas, and the truck will move more quickly,'' he instructed.

Serena mashed the gas, and the truck shot backward.

"Stop!" Cade cried.

"Aieee!" Serena shrieked.

Cade jerked her leg off the accelerator, kicking his boot over her foot and onto the brake. The truck came to a sudden stop, so swiftly that Serena was certain her teeth had flown out of her head. Adrenaline flowed through her, making her gasp.

"I think I need practice!" She glanced at her husband as he shifted the gear into Park.

He closed his eyes and leaned his head back against the headrest. His dark skin stretched tight with tension over his high cheekbones.

"Do you agree that I need more practice?" she asked uncertainly. "Or are you angry?"

Opening his eyes, he stared at her, his eyes dangerous obsidian. "I'm not angry, and yes, I do agree that you need more practice. But you also need proper instruction and more information than I gave you. The whiplash I just received alerts me to the fact that I assumed you were asking for lessons in driving a truck, not lessons in driving generally. My apologies."

"I've always had a driver," she explained, "and at Radcliffe University we walked, of course, or sometimes I was allowed to go in a friend's car if there was room for one of my bodyguards."

"I bet you didn't have a whole lot of dates, considering they knew they'd get their hands broken if they tried anything.''

''I had no dates. I had studies,'' she said demurely.

He smiled at her, and her heart fluttered. More than fluttered. It bounced with a whiplash all its own.

''You were probably a great student, Serena. The last thing I could ever call you is stupid.''

''I was merely trying to get your goad.''

For a moment, he stared at her. ''Goat.''

''Pardon?''

''You got my goat.''

She nodded. ''Well, I am glad you are willing to admit that you were wrong, Cade. You do not like to admit when you have been pigheaded, you know.''

He groaned. ''Okay, you got my goad—you won. Now, I've never taught anyone to drive before,'' he admitted. ''Mac and I both learned from the cowboys, and Jessica learned by sneaking out and stealing their trucks to drive around the pastures at night.''

''Did she really do that?'' Serena breathed, trying to imagine such audacity.

''Oh, Jessica's her own individual, from her mismatched eyes to her sassy temper,'' Cade said fondly.

''I wondered about her eyes, but I didn't want to

say anything. There were a couple of women in the harem who had eyes of different colors, and they were quite prized.''

''Don't tell Jessica,'' Cade said dryly. ''She won't appreciate knowing that a man might 'prize' her more because of it. She was fascinated when colored contacts came out so she could choose one color or the other if she wanted.''

He chuckled, and Serena smiled.

''Come on. Let's at least get you to the end of the driveway,'' Cade said abruptly. ''First, put the truck in Drive this time, and we'll circle around on the grass. You might find driving easier if we go forward so you can see where you're going.''

Serena heard the patience in her husband's tone and tried harder to concentrate on the driving lesson than on *him*.

CADE BREATHED a sigh of relief when Serena reached the One Horse Drive-Up without further mishap. She pulled into the parking slot neatly and switched off the truck.

''I am learning,'' she said. ''You are a better teacher than you give yourself credit for.''

He read the menu with one eye since his head was throbbing. ''You're doing great, Serena. There are a couple of things we should discuss, however. You can't drive in the city because you don't have a license. I mean, it's one thing for you to drive around the ranch for fun, but take tonight, for instance. If we got stopped by the police, I'd have some explaining to do.''

"You would simply tell them that you are a prince, and that you can drive wherever you desire," she stated. "Oh, no, that won't work because you don't want to act like a prince."

"Right. But not only that, Serena, it wouldn't be right to say it in the first place. No one should bend the laws of the country that have been put into place for the safety of all—no matter who they are.''

"So what's the point of being royal?"

He grinned at her. "That's why I've never missed being able to claim my title. It wouldn't change who I am fundamentally.''

"In my country, royalty lives much better than others," she said thoughtfully.

"But wouldn't it be ideal if everybody had an equitable standard of living? No poverty, no slums?''

"Equitable standard of living means there would be no royalty, and who would rule?"

"I'm not saying that there shouldn't be a royal family," he said, examining the menu and not really paying attention to the concern in Serena's voice. When he opened both eyes, his headache increased. Maybe if he could talk Serena into letting him drive the truck home, the headache would go away. He was pretty certain it was fear of the unknown that was causing him tension. With Serena driving, he definitely felt he was hanging on to the cliffside of life. He rubbed his forehead, trying to explain with half an attention span. ''I'm saying I don't think of myself as a prince, and I'm happy. I don't try to get out of driving tickets because of who I am. Everyone should take the consequences for their actions.''

''I see,'' Serena said softly. ''Yes, I think you have a point.''

''I think I'll have the double burger,'' Cade said. ''All this driver's ed is making me hungry. Or nervous enough to burn off my breakfast faster.''

He glanced at Serena but she didn't smile. ''What? What did I say? I'm not really all that nervous. You did great.''

She gazed at him. ''Thank you. You're a good teacher.''

Cade liked hearing that she thought so. ''You're a decent pupil. And a beautiful one, besides.''

Even when she rolled her eyes at him, he thought she was beautiful.

''There is so much about you that I don't know,'' she said wistfully.

''And I you,'' he returned. ''Like, how offended will you be if I don't have them cut the onions on my burger?''

A reluctant smile hovered at her lips. ''You don't kiss me often anyway. Why would I even notice?''

Surprise jolted through him. "I have kissed you, though."

"You are slow to do so and have to be encouraged."

"Are you complaining? Or commenting?"

"Complaining."

His gaze naturally went to her lips, which were full and deep peachy with a faint shine. Light paprika highlights sparkled in her hair as the sun came through the window and her skin glowed with a healthy polish. Her straight, tiny nose always looked regal because she challenged him on everything, giving her whole posture, including her nose, a rather saucy, upturned tip. There was even a challenge in her voice right now, disguised in her complaint, and her eyes held the unmistakable fire of the righteous attitude she held.

"I don't even like onions," he said, thinking that he could skip the burger, too, if she wanted to just sit in the car and neck. "Unless they're cooked."

"And kissing?"

"With the right woman," he replied, knowing that would get a response from her.

"I am the right woman," she told him, her tone imperious. "You knew it when you decided to impersonate your brother. Do not keep trying to pull the string away from me. I am not a cat to follow it."

He laughed, reaching to touch her satiny hair with

one gentle finger. "You are such a princess. I don't think you can erase that from one single inch of your royal person."

"You did it without regrets," she said. "I mean to stay here with my husband. I can be a cowgirl instead of a royal." Her nose tilted even more dangerously as she stared at him, making certain he had understood her words clearly. Then she turned to the order box and pressed the button.

"May I help you?" the order taker asked.

"Yes. Prepare me two hamburgers at once without onions," she commanded.

Cade put his chin down on his hand so his princess wouldn't see him laugh.

"Sure, honey," the order taker replied, her voice implying that she hadn't appreciated the peremptory demand. "Would you like that served to you on a silver platter?"

Cade recognized the tone coming over the speaker as someone who had known everybody in Bridle from the time they were in diapers and didn't take guff from anyone.

"Yes, that will be fine," Serena answered.

"Is there anything else I can get Your Highness?" the waitress asked sarcastically.

"How did she know it was me?" Serena glanced at Cade, puzzled.

He shrugged. "I think she's trying to make a point."

Serena frowned. "What point?"

"She didn't like the way you placed your order."

"What does that have to do with her addressing me by my title?"

Sighing, he said, "She's being testy because she thinks you ordered her to get your lunch."

"I did. That's what I'm supposed to do. Order lunch."

"Yes, but in Bridle, we don't really order. We've all known each other for years, or at least known someone who knows someone else, so we request politely and maybe even ask after the kids," he explained as gently as he could.

"I see," Serena said. "I am sorry that I have offended the custom." She leaned back to the microphone. "Pardon me," she said, her tone contrite.

"Yes?" The woman was in no way appeased.

"If we could also have two sodas, that would be very nice. And I was wondering how your children are doing."

Cade clapped his hand over his forehead.

"Who *is* this?" the woman demanded.

"Princess Serena Wilson-Al Farid," Serena said. "And whom do I have the pleasure of addressing, please?"

"Queen Polly Ann Smith Dorchester Smith, because I married my first husband again after my second husband kicked the bucket. I didn't include my maiden name in my title because it's a mouthful. I'll have your silver platter right out to ya, honey.''

The voice went away. Serena looked back to Cade happily. ''She was still being testy when she said she was a queen, but you were correct, she appreciated the courtesy of the inquiry. I didn't realize that there was social protocol to be observed. I will remember to always ask after the family of the person to whom I am speaking.''

He couldn't help falling a little bit under her spell. The glow in her eyes was too alluring, the delight in her tone too compelling. If he was on her turf in Balahar, he'd be making mistakes and gaffes all over the place. ''You're doing fine, Serena.''

''I am trying, my husband.''

The waitress came out to the car carrying a red tray lined with silver foil. ''It's kinda slow, honey, so I took the time to make this humble plastic tray as royal as I could,'' she said with a raised brow.

Serena nodded. ''Your efforts are appreciated.''

Polly Ann looked more closely at Serena. ''Hey, haven't I seen you somewhere?''

Cade pulled his hat down over his eyes, leaned forward and slipped the waitress a twenty. ''We're in a bit of a hurry, so keep the change.''

Serena took the hamburgers and drinks off the tray and handed them to Cade, before switching on the car engine.

''I am learning to drive in America,'' she told the

waitress kindly. "I have never done so before, so you might want to step back onto the curb. I almost ran through a fence before I got here."

Polly Ann jumped back onto the curb, the silver paper on the tray fluttering in the breeze. She stared at Serena as she neatly put the truck in reverse, then just as Serena shifted into Drive and moved away from the parking spot, the woman's mouth rounded in an O of recognition.

Cade grinned, his headache starting to recede for some reason. "I like being with you," he told Serena. "I honestly didn't realize how much I could enjoy doing simple things like going to a drive-up with a woman."

"Not just any woman," Serena reminded him as she blithely rolled a stop sign. "Me."

A loud siren blared behind them. Cade shook his head, regretfully wrapping the burger back into the silver foil. "And then again..." he said with a sigh.

Chapter Fourteen

"Hey there," Officer Duncan Peterson said, leaning on the car window to gaze at Serena. "Howdy, Cade," he continued as an afterthought, clearly smitten by the driver of the truck.

"Duncan," Cade said with a slightly embarrassed nod. Serena had ignored that stop sign as if it were invisible! "My friend is learning to drive, and I guess I glossed over the part about making sure the car stops completely at stop signs."

"You can turn right on red," Duncan told Serena, his tone admiring, "but you must *stop* first. So, I saw your picture in the paper, Princess. How do you like Bridle so far?"

"It's lovely—" Serena began.

"Excuse me," Cade interrupted. "I'm sure you've got a heavy workload today, Duncan. Don't you want to write me a ticket?"

"Nah. It's not every day a man gets to meet a real princess. So, what's a princess like you doing with a guy like him anyway?'' Duncan asked, his tone teasing and his remark aimed at riling Cade.

Duncan's down-home ease with Serena annoyed Cade to no end—not that he was jealous.

''How is your family?'' Serena inquired.

The officer raised his eyebrows as he stared at her. ''They're all fine, sweetheart. Thanks for asking. Has Cade been telling you about my rascals?''

''No. I just met Polly Ann Smith Dorchester Smith at the drive-up and Cade explained to me that it is courteous in Bridle to inquire about everyone's families.''

Duncan shook his head. ''How did you manage to meet this doll?'' he asked Cade, not caring what she learned from Polly Ann or anyone else. ''As a word of caution from an old friend, don't blow this one. As I recall, you couldn't establish a commitment to save your soul after Penny Dearing dumped you.''

Serena turned her head to examine Cade. ''I do not know Penny Dearing.''

Duncan laughed. ''She moved up north with a rich fellow not too many years ago, right after deciding that Cade didn't have deep enough pockets, I guess. Funny when you think about that one, isn't it, Cade? You hanging out with a real princess and all? Bet you wish Penny could see you now.''

Serena frowned. ''But Kadar is a pr—''

"Could we just have the ticket?" Cade interrupted.

"Penny wasn't near as pretty as you are, though," Duncan continued. "Considering all the times I saw Cade making out with that gal when he was here on college breaks, I'd bet you can't pull him off your face, sweetie."

Cade could feel his wife's intense attention burning his face. "Could we please have a ticket?" he demanded. "So you can get back to work?"

Serena turned back to Duncan. "Cade feels that everyone should be treated equally, regardless of their station in life. Please give him a ticket for my driving error, as well as the fact that of course I have no license, and anything else you can think of that I might have done."

Duncan grinned at her. "I've never seen two people more eager to get written up, Princess. But I'm going to have to let you off the hook today. With you being new to our country and all, I wouldn't feel good about it. We want you to be happy here in Bridle, even if you are stuck with this ol' hombre. That's punishment enough."

Cade sighed. "Thanks, Duncan. We really shouldn't keep you any longer from maintaining law and order at the coffeehouse and the pizza restaurant."

"That's all right. I can't wait to tell the wife who I met today. Your picture in the paper didn't do you justice," he complimented Serena. "It was an honor to meet you."

Serena beamed at him. "And I am honored to make your acquaintance as well."

"When you run out of patience with Cade, you call the local high school for driving lessons. They offer courses for folks to brush up on their skills."

"Thank you, Officer Peterson."

"My pleasure, Princess."

The policeman did everything but bow as he patted Serena on the shoulder and backed away from their truck. Cade grunted with annoyance. "Duncan is a numbskull, although a nice one."

She looked thoughtful. "I cannot understand why a woman would marry anyone other than you if she had the chance. Considering your family and The Desert Rose, it is a good arrangement for any woman..." She looked at him for a moment, shyly. "And then there is you, which, when you are not being stubborn, is the very best part of the marriage arrangement for a woman. At least that is my opinion."

They sat silently for a moment before Serena straightened. "I will know at once why you could not stay off Penny Dearing's face and have to be dragged to kiss mine."

Cade shook his head. "That was a few years back. I'd forgotten all about her until Duncan mentioned her."

"Oh," Serena said, her tone somewhat mollified. "I didn't like hearing that you'd kissed another woman, but if you'd forgotten about her—"

"I did. I had." Cade wanted clear of this subject immediately.

"Then kiss me," Serena demanded.

"Now?" They'd nearly gotten a citation, and the princess wanted to smooch.

Then again, it wasn't all that bad an idea, Cade decided, staring at her twinkling eyes and bright smile. "You know, I think you like living on the edge, Serena."

"*Now,* Prince Kadar," she reiterated, puckering. "Otherwise I will have to again bring up the unfortunate Penny Dearing, who passed up a true prince to marry a rich man and move away up north."

"All right," he said, leaning to frame her face with one hand as he drew her close to him. The feeling of Serena's lips molding to his sent heat into regions of his body he'd let grow cold over time. She warmed his heart; she warmed his life.

Maybe, he thought as she slid her fingers through the hair on the back of his nape, *maybe I could sit here all day and kiss this lady.*

Behind them, the siren wailed again. Serena and Cade jumped apart as if they'd been snapped by static.

They poked their heads out of opposite truck windows to stare back at Duncan, who was waving from the cruiser. Using the speaker, he said, "You two can't sit there and obstruct traffic. I'll have to give you a ticket for that."

"Start the engine," Cade tersely said. "Let's get home."

Home. It was the first time he'd thought of The Desert Rose as home for him and Serena as a married couple. Suddenly the pieces in his life shifted, and instead of thinking that she might want to leave Bridle in a few days, he was hoping that she'd want to stay with him.

Somehow, she had become his home.

THE SECOND SERENA PULLED into The Desert Rose driveway, she panicked and threw the truck into a grinding halt. She had good reason to panic, because reporters swarmed the truck, snapping pictures and thrusting microphones through the open window.

"Did you know your marriage isn't legal, Princess?" a reporter asked.

"Why are you hiding who you really are, Prince Kadar?" another one demanded. "Why are you hiding out here in Bridle, Texas?"

Serena glanced to Cade, horrified. "I told no one," she said on a gasp. "I promise you I did not."

"Drive close to the house, up on the yard," he instructed tersely. "We'll make a run for it from there."

"But they are blocking the way!"

"They'll move."

She forced the truck forward slowly and reporters reluctantly eased out of the path. Suddenly they heard the familiar blare of a police siren behind them.

Duncan got out of the cruiser with a bullhorn. "Ya'll are on private property. Move away from the truck, and find yourselves a place down the lane to park. Any pictures taken closer than the sign posted that says Private Drive will be considered evidence that you have trespassed on private property."

The reporters mumbled, not of a mind to listen.

"They're not going to talk to you," he continued. "Whereas maybe if you haul yourselves a safe distance away, the family might be talked into a press conference at some point."

"Drive while he's got their attention," Cade said swiftly. "Park on the lawn next to the steps."

She did, her hands trembling on the steering wheel as she told herself she could do this, she could drive close to the house without hitting any of the pretty landscaping.

"That'a girl," Cade said. "Now put it in Park and let's get inside."

She did as he asked, and they both jumped out of the truck, hurrying onto the porch.

"Thanks, Duncan," Cade called.

"Forgot to tell you your mom had called to ask

if there was anything to be done about the reporters. I'll handle 'em.''

Cade waved his thanks but didn't hang around long enough to see the "handling." Rose held the door open, closing it behind them as Serena and Cade came through. "Somehow," she said simply, "they found out that the princess is not your wife in proper name."

"I wonder who could be behind that." Cade didn't like his short time with Serena being the object of the world's scrutiny.

Serena and Rose glanced at each other.

"Layla," they said together.

"Why? Why this plan? What does it accomplish for her?" he asked.

"She brings us out of hiding, and with a media spotlight turned on this awkward position between you and Serena, she is hoping that the country of Sorajhee will feel that King Zak is not being honest with them. That there is a reason he had his daughter married in secret. Remember that there has been unrest between the two countries lately. Layla and Azzam are heating the situation to a boiling point. King Zak and I had hoped that a royal marriage between Serena and Prince Makin would be satisfactory to the people, as Makin is the son of Ibrahim, whom the people of Sorajhee had loved."

"But because the marriage didn't go off as

planned, and since it isn't even legal, the people are suspicious,'' Cade finished.

"Not to mention that Layla will be at the ready, sending out her teams of well-versed gossipmongers to spread lies to increase the people's tension,'' Rose explained. "It is a difficult problem we have unwittingly brought to the king, Kadar.''

"Have you spoken to my father?'' Serena asked.

"Not as yet. The press only just arrived, so none of this has had a chance to hit the world airwaves.'' Rose shook her head sadly. "When I think of all the years Randy and Vi protected us, kept your very existence a secret, it makes me want to tear every hair from Layla's wicked head. She has gone too far now.''

"Mother.'' Cade put an arm around his mother's shoulders and gave her a squeeze. "Somehow we'll make all this work out.''

"Perhaps it is best if I return home now,'' Serena said softly. "My presence has caused enough trouble already.''

"Absolutely not,'' Cade and Rose said in unison.

"No matter what, I am determined that Layla will not force you and Cade to make decisions you will regret for the rest of your lives,'' Rose said. "Unless this latest dilemma changes your father's mind, you have yet a week at The Desert Rose if you want to stay, Serena.''

Serena looked at Cade, wondering what she

would see in his eyes. Did he really want her to stay? Or was it merely his pride that was talking?

"You are not going, Serena," he said, shocking her. "You don't move one inch from The Desert Rose until you tell me you want to go. And then I will fly you back to Balahar myself."

"I fear I am trouble to you—"

"Nonsense," Rose denied. "I didn't spend years in a sanitarium by Layla's treachery to give up this easily. I learned survival, and I learned determination. I side with Prince Kadar in his decision. If you both want the last few days that King Zak has granted, then we will not allow Layla to take that from you."

"I want it," Serena whispered, her eyes on Cade. "If my prince wishes it, Prince Kadar."

"I have already made my decision," he said imperiously. "You stay here with us."

Sweet shivers ran all over Serena's body. There was fire in Prince Kadar's eyes, glowing for her. She felt his possession of her heart in full flame, and told herself she would walk through the worst fire Layla could conjure before leaving her prince.

IN BALAHAR, King Zak opened the letter put in front of him by an adviser. It was from Rose Coleman, and he very much looked forward to her missive. He wanted to learn how the courtship was progressing; he trusted Rose had been correct in believing that Serena and Kadar were not totally immune to each other.

But it was the photograph that fell out from between the pages that caught his eye.

The photo showed Rose Coleman with her three sons—and Rose was as lovely as he remembered. He smiled at the classic image reminiscent of Princess Grace of Monaco. Soft upswept blond hair complemented a bone structure that was aging gracefully. Her eyes held laughter, her mouth curved in a smile as her sons stood proudly on either side of her. Her son Alex he thought quite handsome. Kadar and Makin he couldn't tell apart, though he suspected he recognized the arrogant stance of Kadar, feet apart, independent even though he stood protectively near his mother.

On the back of the photograph, Rose's slanting penmanship confirmed his guess. All of her sons looked strong and virile, but King Zak decided he was glad Serena had chosen Kadar, even by accident. He was strong and determined, and he would need that to deal with Serena. She was very much like her stepbrother, Sharif.

That thought made King Zak flip the photo back over to stare more closely at Rose's sons. He pulled a photo from his desk of Sharif and Serena and himself, putting the two close together so he could inspect them.

If he didn't know better, he would think that Sharif had Rose's classic bone structure. His imagination could be working overtime, but possibly Sharif's stance even mimicked that of the other princes. The eyes were similar, fierce with pride.

His mouth dropped open. It simply could not be.

He remembered the baby that had been brought to him and Nadirah for adoption. His wife had said the child was the son of parents who had died. It was the year Ibrahim had been killed in an assassination attempt done right, although no one had ever learned who was behind the deed. Rose had disappeared with her children. Zak had become busy over the next nine months, as he learned how to keep peace with the new king, Azzam. Too preoccupied to question his wife's wish to finally have a child of her own, he had granted her wish to keep the orphaned infant. He wanted someone around him to be happy, and he'd been relieved to provide her with a child, since he could not.

He had never considered treachery.

Surely his mind was merely imagining this, craving a connection of some kind to family since he no longer had the wife he loved. Or maybe he was at last getting old and his eyes played tricks on him.

Even a man's heart played tricks on him in his twilight years, bringing him wistful memories from the past. Sometimes changing him, mellowing him.

He examined the picture again, comparing Rose to her sons, and then to Sharif.

It was not possible.

But he'd been forged by the intrigues of royalty for too long not to at least give his suspicion some consideration.

He looked at the picture again, his gaze now only on her.

She was a beautiful woman. Despite what the papers had said when Ibrahim had married Rose Coleman and decided to have only her, forsaking a harem, it was clear the deceased king had chosen well.

He wondered if the men in Texas were vying to keep the widowed ex-queen company—and decided he found that thought strangely unsettling.

Chapter Fifteen

"This is my fault you have been discovered," Serena said to Cade and Mac as they sat at the kitchen table. "I am embarrassed to have caused this trouble to you."

"If it's anyone's fault, it's mine," Mac said. "I sent my brother to check you out. If I'd done my duty, we'd be married well and good by now. And there'd be nothing Layla and Azzam could do about it."

Cade watched Serena's and Mac's eyes meet in consternation. He grinned as they both instantly shook their heads in the negative.

"I am sorry, Prince Makin—" Serena began.

"Well, I'm not," Mac said. "What my brother did for a favor to me is turning out to be right for him, no matter how difficult it seems right now. You two are meant to be together."

"We'll have to outthink the problem," Cade said. Serena was all his woman, destined to be his—if he could just figure out a way to make it happen on his terms.

He snapped his fingers. "I'm taking you home," he told Serena.

"What?" she asked, her eyes suddenly filling with tears. "Do not send me back to Balahar, my prince! I would stay here with you, and not cause you trouble, although I know I will cause you some with driving lessons and other things my temper gets me into. But otherwise I will be a good wife!"

Shaking his head, he said, "I need to face this head-on, Serena. It's the only way."

"You will end up assassinated like your father," she said bitterly. Instantly, she gasped. "I am sorry! I should not have spoken so!"

Cade's eyes narrowed on his wife. "What makes you think I would be assassinated?"

"Because you have married me," she said miserably. "And that puts you in line for the throne, no matter how much you do not want it. You can rule, because you are not a commoner by birth, as I am. Only Crown Prince Sharif would be before you, and any children he may ever have."

"Your father will arrange his marriage next, and considering what you have told me about the ladies vying for his…what was it?" he asked Serena.

"Favor."

"Right. Favor. No doubt his wife will do the same. They can have a bundle of babies, and I'm in the clear.'' Cade shook his head. ''That's no reason for me to fear returning.''

''It doesn't have to have a reason!'' Serena exclaimed. ''Nipping off the buds of the plant assures that no new growth lives!''

''Whoa,'' Mac said. ''You don't want to be nipped, Cade. Maybe I should go with you as your bodyguard.''

''I'm supposed to be Serena's, but she makes it difficult,'' Cade grumbled good-naturedly. ''I don't think having both of us over there at the same time would be good for Mother's state of mind.''

''There is that,'' Mac agreed.

''Serena and I will have to go alone. We will remarry with my name in a ceremony that the people can see, so that they can stop worrying about their king's political choices.''

''You were not a political choice,'' Serena said. ''I came with you of my own free will, without asking my father's permission, even though I had discovered you were an imposter. That makes this a match between equals. I am your choice, and you are mine,'' Serena said. ''But I think we should stay here and get married, if that is your wish. I do not want you in harm's way, Kadar.''

''We marry in Balahar,'' Cade stated. ''And invite Layla to come drink some wedding punch, preferably poisoned.''

''Cade!'' Mac said with a laugh. ''You're becoming royal after all, if you're going to start planning intrigues.''

"Fight fire with fire,'' Cade said. "Serena, don't tell your father we're coming. This visit is going to be a surprise.''

"I do not want you to go,'' Serena said. "I forbid it, my prince. I will return alone. I will not marry you if you do this. It is unsafe, and I would rather be a concubine here in Texas than married in Balahar!'' She burst into tears.

Cade gaped at his wife. "A concubine? Have you lost your mind? I promised your father I would not dishonor you, and I can tell you right now, lovely princess, *I keep my promises*. Besides which, my father did not keep a harem, a fact that scandalized his country, particularly when he did not marry his betrothed, Layla. I sure as hell am not going to break with tradition. Now get packed,'' he said, angered.

Serena flew from the room, her weeping audible.

"Do you think you're a little hard on her?'' Mac asked. "She's trying to protect you.''

"Yeah, well, I don't have to hide behind her gauzy little skirts,'' Cade stated. "I'll do the protecting. I don't think a minor prince is going to cause much of a threat to the throne, especially this prince who's made no secret that he'll be spending his life right here at The Desert Rose.''

Mac raised an eyebrow at him. "You're beginning to sound more and more royal all the time. Do you remember when you used to be a fun-loving guy who never took anything seriously? In fact, the whole reason you went to Balahar in the first place was to protect me, because you said my heart wasn't easy-come easy-go enough to enter into a marriage of convenience.''

''I don't have time for yakking, Mac. Serena has fit herself into my world, and done her best to learn to love Texas. The least I can do is return the favor in some small measure. She left her home with little more than a hairbrush. I'll take her back and we'll do this thing right, for once and for all.''

''Don't you mean, for better or for worse?''

''It's definitely got to get better,'' Cade said, heading upstairs to pack, ''because in no way do I intend to allow it to get worse.''

''WHERE'S SERENA?'' Cade asked his mother an hour later. He'd filed a flight plan, gotten some clothes together. But now he couldn't find his wife.

Rose stared at her son. ''She is determined not to go to Balahar where you will be in danger, so she has left.''

''Left…what?''

''This house.''

''You let her?'' He was incredulous.

''She is a princess,'' Rose replied in surprise. ''She has a mind of her own. I know that Vi and Randy would not have raised you in my absence to be a chauvinist, Kadar, so I'm assuming your attitude has more to do with dismay that she has gone rather than annoyance that she operates under her own principles.''

''Considering the circumstances of a hundred reporters outside our gates, I'm merely expressing concern that you would advise Serena to go,'' Cade said, not happy at all to hear that Serena wasn't falling in with his plans easily.

''I did not advise her to go,'' Rose told him sternly. ''This is not a prison, however. She is free to come and go as she pleases—and it is not her wish to return to her country. I must counsel you to listen to your wife's feelings, Kadar. Not listening is a mistake that ruins many a young marriage. A good foundation can be set for life if the two partners will listen to each other in the early days of the union.''

''I have Serena's best interest at heart.''

''But she does not find it to be her best interest, and she felt you would pressure her to return. This is a crossroads you must fix between you, but I must reiterate that this is not a time to be overbearing,'' Rose warned.

''I am never overbearing,'' Cade said.

''I suggest you find your wife and ask her whether she finds you so and, moreover, if she wishes to return. Please listen to her answer. Flight plans can be refiled and suitcases can be repacked, but the foundation of a solid marriage is poured once in the beginning and will be lived with forever.'' Rose swept from the room.

"Great,'' Cade muttered. "Females aligned against me is a bad sign. This has never happened before in my life. Never.''

"I heard that,'' Rose said, poking her head back into the room. "If you take your bruised pride down to the guest house, you will find your wife and all the privacy you need, if you don't let the press see you.''

"Thanks, Mother.'' Cade saluted his mother with a relieved smile.

"Well, I said she was free to go of her own free will, but I didn't let her get far,'' Rose said with a dry smile. "I am my son's mother, after all, and I want him to have the woman he loves, even if he is slow in the love department.''

"Slow in the love department!''

"The romance department, as well,'' Rose added. "Remember, this princess loves you, Cade.''

"Loves...me?'' he echoed, realizing for the first time that neither of them had ever spoken those words. He wanted her, he would possess her, he would keep her forever, but he had not expected to love her. Nor to have her love in return. "Did she say that?''

Rose shook her head. "No, and I do not suspect she will tell you that she does today, either. You have upset her greatly. Be patient, Kadar, and all good things will eventually come to you.''

''Patience isn't my strongest suit, but I'll try.''

His mother disappeared from the room.

But before he could find his princess, it was too late.

SERENA STARED in horror at the television in the guest house as one of the news programs flashed a picture of her in her apron on the TV screen. That wasn't nearly as bad as the next shots of her learning to drive, and then pulling up in front of the house, grinding to a bone-jarring stop. There were pictures of her wearing jeans and raking stalls, and pitch-forking fresh hay into other stalls.

Cade, of course, they only showed watching her in his customary position of arms crossed over his chest, legs spread, as if instructing her to work like an indentured servant.

But the worst part was the TV anchor speaking about them as if they had no feelings, as if they were merely any other news item.

''It seems ironic to have a princess living among us, it is even more ironic that we have had a queen for months and not known it,'' the anchor said. ''After spending several years in a sanitarium in Europe, Queen Rose Coleman-El Jeved returned to the States—''

"Oh, no!" Serena exclaimed. "They make her sound like a crazy woman!"

"Yes, they do," came Cade's grim voice from behind her. She gasped, whirling. "I did not hear you come in!"

"I didn't knock. I walked in, hoping that no photographers had followed me. I don't think I tipped them off. I rode Texas Heat as fast as he could gallop once I left the main grounds. I think we are safe from their lenses here."

"We are not safe anywhere," Serena said bitterly. "They have made me appear to be abused and downtrodden and kidnapped by your hand. My people will be outraged. Layla has done her work well."

"We can explain—"

"We cannot explain the fact that they know a marriage took place but it was false. There is no changing the way that looks, Kadar. It did not occur to me the disaster we would wreak by not revealing your identity. By my own decision, I have hurt my father, and I have hurt my country."

"At the time we thought—"

She whirled on him. "It does not matter what we thought at the time. That is the fishbone of all rulers that sits constantly at the top of their throats and threatens to be swallowed. Every decision is a fishbone, and if it turns out well, then it does not choke them. But if it is a bad decision, even an error in the wisest ruler's judgment, then..." She looked at him with anguished, haunted eyes. "It's not just my family and my country that have been hurt. Your mother will be heartbroken to have the world know she was in a sanitarium for years. And the only person who knew this was Layla," she said angrily. "I know Layla arranged to have your father killed, because Azzam is too weak to care whether he sits on a throne or not."

"There is nothing I can do about that situation now. It is done and in the past. But we shouldn't allow Layla to manipulate us."

"She has from the moment we laid eyes on each other. It was the reason we married without revealing who you were, because I was afraid of Layla discovering there was a hitch in the wedding plans. You said you did not want to jump to Layla's commands, but that is exactly what has happened." It made her sad to realize how effectively Layla's circle had closed upon her. Like a well-oiled trap, it had sprung shut with steel teeth.

Cade ran a hand through his hair. "I have to think about this for a few moments. I'm not used to plotting at this level."

"It's not something you can learn to do overnight. Besides which, the end result is that the people are already outside the palace protesting the fact that my father has not brought me back. This is bordering on an international incident, Kadar,'' Serena said sadly.

"Surely no one will believe that I kidnapped you!''

"Another king's wife says you did. I left hurriedly, without so much as my own clothes. What princess does that?''

He shook his head. "I don't care what they think. None of it's true.''

"Right. In history courses at university, we learned that several conspiracy theories exist in the United States, which grow over time to be more believed than the actual proven truth.'' She put her hands on her hips. "What makes you think the same does not exist in other countries? Balaharians are *used* to thinking about conspiracies, Kadar, because palace intrigue has always been a fact of life. No one is going to believe anything you and I say.''

He shook his head, angry and helpless in the face of a situation from which he could not protect her. "So what do you suggest we do?''

She took a deep breath. "There is only one course of action. I must return to my home.''

"You said you didn't want to go back!''

Her eyes met his, as brown flashed against deep green pools of unhappiness. "I am a princess, Kadar. What I want to do and what I do are two different things.''

"You are not in Balahar now, Serena.''

Her smile was slight and accepting of her fate. "Ask your mother about her life, Kadar. Ask her if there were ever times she did what she had to do versus what she wanted to do."

"She would not want you to leave me, I know that."

Serena nodded. "I know. She did not want Ibrahim assassinated. She did not want her sons in jeopardy. She did not want to be incarcerated in a sanitarium. But all these things came to her, and she dealt with them. As I will deal with this dilemma, as well." Searching his face for understanding, she said, "Kadar, I am asking you to take me home. You said, if I ever asked you, you would take me back immediately. Now, I am asking for that very thing."

Chapter Sixteen

Cade felt as though a boulder had just been heaved against his chest. He was caught between his promise to Serena, and the pain of giving her up. Once he took her back to Balahar, he knew he would never see her again.

"No," he said stubbornly. "That isn't the answer, unless I go with you. But I'm not dropping you off like a container of milk, if that's what you're asking."

"Then I will fly on a commercial plane." Her chin rose. "And I will be gone before you or the press ever knows I have left The Desert Rose."

"Now, look here, Princess," Cade began, but Serena cut him off.

"No, you look here. Our marriage was supposed to bring stability to my country, to satisfy the people that the rule of my father is ongoing and secure. This has not happened. This was an arrangement, Kadar, and sometimes arrangements do not work out."

"It *was* working fine."

"Not really, because you and I never became compatible."

He stared at her. "What the hell are you talking about?"

She turned her back. "You know very well."

"Wait a minute, Princess. I can only speak for myself, but I think we're very compatible. We've been hamstrung by this royalty problem since the word *go,* however, and—"

"We'll be hamstrung by it forever, Kadar. Don't you see that? I am what I am, and you are what you are. You have spent many years being shielded from the heat of being a prince. But you can no longer ignore it. You must make decisions that are unerring and unselfish."

He was a man. He liked simplified details. What was he supposed to do? Allow this woman to fly out of his life without a protest?

"It would be best if we parted amicably without causing further distress between us," Serena said, her voice gentle, her back still turned. "I do not wish to remember you awkwardly."

His brows shot up into his hair. "You are not going to have to remember me at all, because you are going to be living under my roof, as my wife, until the day we draw our last breaths."

"I am not your wife now, Prince Kadar, and there isn't anything you could say to make me change that fact. My people are unhappy with our alliance. I will not do anything further to upset them.''

He had forgotten that one tiny detail. They were not legally married, and he'd been determined that if Serena wanted to leave him in the two weeks her father had granted them, she would return to her father in the condition he had promised.

Untouched.

''I'm caught in my own good intentions,'' he said with dawning realization. ''We wouldn't even be discussing the bizarre idea of you returning if I'd made love to you day and night like I wanted to.''

Now she turned around to face him. ''I do not believe you on that score, Prince Kadar. You didn't get within two feet of me without me scheming to get there.''

''Well, believe this—certain parts of my anatomy felt like they were bursting because I wanted you so badly. But what could I do? I made a promise.''

''As I have made a promise to the people my father rules. He is a king, Kadar. Everything we do is supposed to benefit the people. While I do thank you for your integrity and honor in keeping me intact—which will be verified by a palace physician— I am going home whether you take me or not.''

Cade's brain couldn't think any faster of how to get them out of the mudslide sucking them down. ''I'm not dumping you off in Balahar,'' he repeated. ''I'll go to the palace with you.''

"That is very heroic, but you will be most likely assassinated, either outside the palace by the people or inside by Layla's spies. Not a course of action your mother would sanction."

"I'll take bodyguards, and I won't eat the food." He shrugged. "You're not going without me."

"Once upon a time I thought you would be a good ruler because you possess determination," Serena stated, her eyes flashing. "But now I see that your stubbornness would be the downfall of you, and maybe anyone under your rule! You cannot always write your own destiny, Kadar. It's bad for the throne when people make decisions that benefit only themselves and hurt other people in the process!"

He threw himself on a sofa and lifted his boots up onto the table, careless of the scarring the heels might cause. Staring at her, he said, "Okay, Princess, tell me exactly what it is that you want me to do. Draw me a map and make it real clear, because I'm more cowboy than prince and I make simple decisions because I rule livestock and not people."

"Now you are angry. You feel I have insulted you." Serena sat down across from him, but she might as well have been in another room as far as Cade was concerned. The gulf between them was widening further all the time.

His gaze was direct. "Let's not worry about my feelings. Let's concern ourselves with what we have to do."

"I have to return home," Serena said slowly. "By myself."

"Our marriage will be, well, hell, it doesn't even have to be annulled, because it was a sham to start with."

"Correct."

"You're off the hook totally, aren't you, Princess?" The pain that shot through Cade's heart was agonizing. "Excuse me, I injected emotions into the conversation," he said sarcastically. "Let me refocus the plans. When would you like to return?"

"Tomorrow? Would that be convenient?" she asked, her delicate face alight with hope that would be etched upon his soul forever. She wanted to go home. He had told her he would take her if she ever decided to go.

"Yes. I can do that," he said, getting up from the sofa. His boots scraped scratches into the table wood as he stood, but Cade didn't notice. The pain in his chest took precedence as he bowed stiffly to his wife. "There are three rooms in this guest house. You may sleep in one, and I will take another. Trust me, Princess, you need have no fear that I will inconvenience you. But you are not sleeping in this guest house without protection—paparazzi and Layla and everyone else be damned. We leave in the morning."

SERENA'S HEART fell apart when her husband stalked out of the room. *No, Kadar is not my hus-*

band, she reminded herself. *That's why you have made the decision to leave him.*

Maybe it seemed cruel to have spoken to him the way she had, but she could see no way out of the problem that encircled them. If he went to Balahar, there was a very real chance he would be killed, and she would not do that to Rose even if Cade thought he could survive anything Layla could throw at him. His father had not—Serena shivered. No. History would not repeat itself on her behalf.

She flipped to CNN, wincing at the pictures of her carrying buckets. Zoom lenses were a curse to anyone who wanted to live a life without intrusion! Glancing at her hands, she saw not the hands of a pampered princess, but one who saddled her own horse, picked horse hooves clean. A burn on the other palm from picking up a too-hot pot. Cade had kissed her hand, she remembered, and she'd insisted that made her feel better than the ice he'd applied right after.

The reminiscent smile slid from her face. Her father had to be completely dismayed by these events. She felt that she had shamed him in some way.

She wasn't the kind of woman who thought a good cry made things better, but she didn't notice the single tear that slipped down her cheek as she went into her bedroom alone.

WITH ABDUL-RAHIM at her side, Layla stared at the photograph her spy, Shadi, had spirited from the palace. After all these years, to see Rose smiling and happy with her grown boys—it was more than Layla could bear. Hatred licked inside her, lighting a flaming fire that had lived on memories for years.

Ibrahim should have been hers. Their families had betrothed them. But Rose Coleman had come along and stolen the prince she should have had, while Layla had to settle for a very lesser prince.

And now Rose was ever closer to her goal. Because no one would miss the resemblance between Sharif and the brothers in the photograph.

"They are very like," Abdul-Rahim murmured.

"Yes." King Zak would remember who had brought that infant for him and his wife to raise. Layla's only hope of being spared was if Azzam should rise to his feet and demand a return of the rule that he had slowly abdicated over the years.

Layla's shoulders slumped. He would not do that for her. He would not even do it for himself. Like a besotted drunkard being plied with his favorite wine, King Zak had been very wise to gift the harem with beautiful nubile young women who kept Azzam *very* satisfied.

Layla threw a perfume bottle across the room, shattering it on the marble floor. She might as well take Cleopatra's out and place an asp to her bosom.

But then Rose wins forever, the voice whispered,

that shepherd of her inner dreams. *Must you live and die unloved?*

Slowly Layla indicated that Shadi should leave the room. He gestured for the photograph, uneasy that he had been gone from Balahar's palace too long.

"You have no need of the photograph, Queen," Abdul-Rahim said.

Ignoring her adviser, she shook her head in the negative. The servant's eyes widened with apprehension. Before their shocked gazes, she tore the picture in four parts and set them in a lit brazier to turn to bright bits of flame.

"King Zak must have misplaced the photograph," she assured the servant. "No one would possibly imagine that I had any interest in it at all. You are safe."

The servant nodded, bowing as he left the room.

Layla knew why Rose had sent the picture to the king. She had known he would see the resemblance, had known she was putting the knife edge to Layla's throat.

It would not matter. Rose, she vowed, would never see the throne of Balahar.

"WE CAME TO SAY GOODBYE," Rose told Serena as a group filed into the guest house. Looking somber, Mac and Jessica, Randy and Vi, entered behind Rose.

"I brought you your suitcase," Jessica offered. "Maybe you'll have the chance to wear all the stuff we bought you one day. Especially the lingerie."

Serena's gaze flashed to Cade before flitting away. *Look all you like,* he thought. *You are not leaving me forever.*

She wanted to be with him, and he knew it. They belonged together. For that reason alone, he would take her back to Balahar. Time would prove to her that there was a way to work out their situation.

He would not agree to an annulment. Serena was his wife and she was staying that way—unless she told him without outside interference that she didn't want to be with him anymore.

As far as he could tell, all that stood between him and Serena was a palace, a country and a scheming old witch.

He could take on those odds.

THE RETURN FLIGHT to Balahar was quiet between them. Cade had arranged for a co-pilot, someone to spell him as they weren't delaying on the way except for fuel when necessary. With a third person aboard, an awkward wall was created, adding to the feeling of estrangement. Common courtesies were observed, but Cade didn't try to change Serena's mind. She was glad, because her dilemma was great enough as it was. The political turmoil facing her country was peaking, her family's rule questioned.

She knew how the newspapers had made her look. Denials would never be believed.

It was best to return home and give up an unpopular marriage—no matter how much it broke her heart to do it. A princess didn't always get exactly what she wanted—that was a fairy-tale myth.

Rose Coleman certainly had not gotten what she had wanted out of life. Extreme suffering had been visited upon her. For Serena to do her duty with less courage and conviction than Rose had shown during her life would be wrong.

On the landing strip, she was met by Sharif, her father, and a palace driver who silently took her single bag. She embraced her father and brother while Cade stood behind her stoically. Tears stung her eyes as she buried her face against her father's chest. "I'm sorry," she whispered.

"Al Hamdo Lillah Ala Al Salamah," was all he said, the traditional Arabic greeting to say that he thanked God for bringing her back safely. But when she looked up she found her father staring at Cade, as if the greeting encompassed him, too. The look on her father's and brother's faces held no animosity, nor criticism. Cade's was blank, as well.

But there was a silent current of communication. To Serena, it felt like a question that was not going to be answered by her husband. Ex-husband. Or never-husband, however one catalogued a left-behind spouse.

Cade's gaze fell to her then, like a laser beam landing on her, deep and dark in intensity. He nodded before reentering the jet. Her father and brother walked her to a waiting limousine and, though she desperately wanted to look back, to run to Cade, she forced herself inside the long car and only allowed herself a glance back at his plane after she was concealed behind the impenetrable windows.

CADE WAITED until the car carrying Serena and her family left the premises, the long slash of black smoothly snaking from the airport road onto an access road. He'd hoped against hope that at the last moment—at any moment—she might change her mind. But she had not. The car left his range of vision. It felt like a deep black hole opened up in his chest.

"Next stop—Saudi Arabia," he told the co-pilot. "The closest place to wait until my wife realizes she doesn't even need a one-way ticket to get home to The Desert Rose."

And home to me.

WHEN LAYLA HEARD that Serena had returned to Balahar without her husband, she smiled. Victory!

Now was the time to secure the throne. With unrest roiling between the states, the logical next step was to suggest a further alliance between them for the sake of domestic relations.

Princess Serena should marry Prince Ali Denarif, distant cousin to Azzam. Even King Zak would have to admit the benefit of cooling the recent storm that Serena's precipitous marriage had caused. She was in disgrace, as well as good as cast off by her Western husband. This would make the bargaining cheap for Layla's side of the transaction, a point that stingy Ali Denarif's family would appreciate. They well knew their son's proclivities did not run to females in general; he had been uneasy about making a marriage that would test him to produce heirs. This match would be appealing to him, because who else would want a headstrong princess that another man did not want? And Layla's country would benefit from this alliance—and thereby, she would be admired for bringing about a favorable resolution for all parties concerned. Not to mention ridding herself of further possible heirs from Serena's branch of the family tree—for her, there would be no children. Marrying Serena to Ali Denarif would be like watching a door irrevocably close, and the very image of that door shutting gave Layla great pleasure.

If no one else remembered the treachery of Rose Coleman, Layla had never forgotten. Layla's loyalty to her country ran more fiercely than a raging river. Had Ibrahim married Layla, his true betrothed, instead of the scheming Rose, he would have reached a greater destiny in his abbreviated life.

However, now her loyalty had to be to her husband, the rightful king. *How rich and well deserved it will be to bargain for Princess Serena for a mere song of quick thinking on my part. One day, Azzam will understand how brilliant I am, and appreciate everything I've done.*

For him.

Chapter Seventeen

"I have received three offers of marriage this very morning," King Zak told Serena with some surprise. "I must admit some astonishment, considering the situation."

"Refuse them all," Serena said listlessly, "if you can, Father. I do not wish to marry again so soon."

She might have an annulled marriage, but in her heart she had been married to Cade. It was impossible to imagine herself with any other.

"I am not eager to encourage you to do that which you do not wish," her father replied. "However, there is one proposal that must receive stringent consideration. Prince Ali Denarif offers the goodwill of his country, and his family, if you will consent to wed with him."

"Prince Ali is a worm, and his family a den of maggots!" Serena said with horror. "You cannot be serious thinking of such an alliance!"

King Zak shook his head. "I only said his proposal bears measured thought. You are as aware as any that one should keep their friends close to them, but keep their enemies closer. Layla and Azzam conspire constantly against us. With a marriage to Denarif, they would feel more appeased.''

''Ugh!'' Serena thought about Jessica and the expressive language her friend would have used if she were in Serena's shoes right now. No one would get Jessica to wed if she did not want to. She smiled, thinking about Kadar's claim that no one would ever marry his bossy cousin with the mismatched eyes.

''You find something amusing, daughter?''

''No,'' she murmured. ''I was just thinking about someone I liked very much.''

''Prince Kadar?''

She shook her head. ''It is not a smile that comes to my face when I think about him. I want to kick him in the pants.''

''That's an interesting way to speak of someone whom you seem quite...unable to forget,'' the king observed wryly.

Blowing out a breath, she said, ''Kadar is an exasperating man, Father. Just when I thought he would not budge an inch, he would willingly give me a mile. But I still want to kick him in the pants.''

''Did you always feel that way?''

She smiled. ''Pretty much. And he felt that way about me as well.''

"Ah, you were well matched, then." The king chuckled.

Serena wrinkled her nose. "I do not know if I would say that, exactly."

"Hmm." The king adjusted his robe and reached for a goblet before saying, "You will not miss him, then."

She put her head down. "He is infuriating."

"I see."

"And arrogant."

"Oh."

"Impossible. Incorrigible. And...well, words cannot describe how I feel about him."

Her father looked at her with concern. "Such strong emotions to be vented upon one hapless male."

"Hapless? Hardly. No, I will not miss him." Serena would not allow herself to miss a man who had not uttered his love for her. He had not wanted to marry her in the first place; he had come to Balahar on an errand for his brother. If he had wanted her, he would have made their marriage a real one. "I will not miss him," she said softly, "but I am not eager to test the waters of marriage again so quickly."

"Your dilemma is known over the world, daughter," her father said gently. "It is best to solve the problem and put the matter behind us."

Serena shuddered. "Not Prince Ali Denarif. He is...he and I would not suit."

"You say you and Prince Kadar did not suit."

"That was different!" Serena exclaimed. "He could be quite stubborn about most everything!"

"Prince Ali will not be stubborn," the king reminded her. "It will be basically a political alliance, as I'm sure you are aware."

Serena closed her eyes. Rose had not wished to languish in a sanitarium as a political pawn, but she had survived it. Jessica did not want mismatched eyes, but she didn't let it bother her unduly. What was a marriage, if the heart was not involved? Merely something she could deal with, as other women dealt with their circumstances as they had to. "Let me think about it for one night, Father."

He patted her hand. "In my heart, I wonder if you did not find Prince Kadar more to your liking than you are willing to admit. You are quite headstrong yourself, Serena."

Kadar had been quite to her liking.

She had not been to his.

And how was that any different from marrying Prince Ali Denarif?

"TELEPHONE, PRINCESS," King Zak's secretary said upon entering the palace garden where Serena was walking, lost in her thoughts.

"Who is it?"

"It is Prince Kadar," the secretary said without change in expression.

Serena's heart fluttered inside her like a freed butterfly. "Where shall I take the call?"

"Inside your father's study would be best."

Serena hurried to the study and picked up the phone. "Hello?"

"Howdy, Princess. I'm just checking to see if you're ready to catch a pony outta here."

She gasped at his audacity. "Where are you?"

"Hanging out in a nearby city. Waiting on you to come to your senses."

Her heart soared, then crashed as she realized that nothing had changed to allow her to accept his offer. "I am glad you called, but I am afraid I have come to my senses."

"Good. I'll swing by and pick you up. We'll be back in Texas before you can blink your eyes and say 'Wow, was that a crazy dream or what?'"

She smiled sadly. "I must stay here, Kadar. But your call has warmed my heart."

"To be honest, I'd rather warm your bed at this point. I've been noble long enough. I'm staying at the Hilton in Penzar if you decide to take me up on the honeymoon we haven't yet had."

He would not make her cry. She would not weep tears of self-pity. "My father has received three offers of marriage. It seems that in my shamed state, I am more sought after than even before."

Several American curse words flowed from Cade's lips. "You are still my wife. I didn't change my mind. You changed yours."

"I cannot change it back now. Where kingdoms are concerned, one must do that which benefits the people most. Imagine how you would feel if your president was not a strong leader. You would surely feel less secure."

"Let's leave politics out of it for now. I hope you're not seriously considering marrying someone else."

"Prince Ali Denarif makes a strong suit for a welcome political alliance. You see, I cannot leave politics out of my life, Kadar. It is not done that way in this country."

"Do you like him?"

Kadar's blunt question brought a wry smile to her face. "Again, you are concerned with the who, when I must think of the what. It is not a matter of whom I like, it is a fact of what I must do to strengthen my father's position and that of my country."

"I asked you if you liked him," Cade said, his voice tight and tense.

"Actually, I do not. He is repugnant to me. But I will be equally repugnant to him, so that is not a concern."

"Is that how it's done in your country? You

marry the person most repugnant to you and live happily ever after?''

She frowned at his sarcasm. "You asked the question. I answered. Do not criticize me, or the way in which we do things. This is not The Desert Rose, where you are the king on your small parcel of land.''

"Small parcel of land!''

"It is not a country, Kadar. It is yours and your family owns it, so you can do as you wish. Here we are servants to the people, something a good king never forgets.''

"Nor does he let his daughter forget it, obviously.''

"Do not assume that words have been put in my mouth,'' she snapped. "I am glad you called, Kadar. I had just told my father how we did not see eye-to-eye on anything. It is good to know that I remembered our brief marriage with clarity.''

"Now wait just a da—''

"Goodbye, Prince Kadar,'' she said, purposefully thumping her fingers hard against the mouthpiece to simulate the noise of a slammed-down receiver.

"Serena?'' he said. "Serena?''

When she didn't answer, he cursed again and hung up.

And just as she had suspected, the very quiet and unmistakable click of another phone hanging up traveled to her ear. Serena allowed herself a dry smile. Prince Kadar had taught her well in Texas, but he had forgotten the lessons he had learned in Balahar before. Spies were a part of life she was used to. She was worried that he had said exactly where he was "hanging out." But she was relieved to have been able to pick an argument with him. The best thing he could do was stay out of Balahar. It was critical that he leave the country as soon as possible.

Her heart banged against her ribs as she thought about the very real risks to him if he remained. Unused to thinking about royal power struggles, he thought only of recapturing what he had obviously decided to keep—her.

He had not considered that his presence would adversely affect the marriage negotiations her father was entertaining. Other suitors would not wish to learn that Kadar was still in the vicinity. Someone on the other end of the phone had learned exactly that. Poison in the food, a fall that came in the darkness, an unlikely vehicle accident; Kadar did not realize how far other people would go to get closer to the throne. As an American male, he thought of her as a woman, a wife, or possibly in his most obstinate moments, a desirable possession; whereas the men who sought her hand now thought of her as a stepping stone.

Kadar did not see her that way because he had no

interest in the throne. She had to send him away, as much as her soul had not wanted to be cruel to him.

But they were no longer in Texas. And they would never be married for real.

"SERENA HAS TOLD CADE he can come on home," Rose told the gathering in the kitchen. "She will not return with him."

"I don't understand why not," Jessica said. "She was crazy about him."

Mac nodded. "I'd have to say I thought Cade wasn't acting quite like his old self once he married Serena. Which, in Cade's case, is a good thing. I've never seen one woman hold his attention the way she did."

Rose shook her head. "I understand her feelings. The paparazzi gave her an unflattering light to live under. She didn't want her father's choice of her husband ridiculed."

"In time, perhaps we could have worked through that," Randy said. He and Vi sat near each other, but not touching the way they had in previous years. "However, the strength in our survival here has been the fact that the family lineage is secure."

"I know Serena felt very guilty that our security had been diminished because of her deceptive marriage to Cade. I can't imagine how that secret got out."

"I can," Rose said. "I'm positive that were we

to dig deep enough, we would find Layla just under the top layer of dirt, hiding from the light.''

''Who is this Prince Ali Denarif Cade says Serena may marry?'' Mac asked.

''He is a cousin of Layla's, and a disgusting excuse for humanity,'' Rose stated. ''She would do better to run away and hide in a jungle rather than marry him. Unfortunately, I can see where the alliance will cool tensions between Balahar and Sorajhee. I understand Serena's predicament all too well, in fact.''

''Will she marry him?'' Jessica asked.

''Of course,'' Rose murmured. ''She will do what she must to help her father, and she also has Sharif to think about. If none of you wishes the throne, then it falls to him.'' She shivered as she remembered the face of the prince in the photograph. If she did not know better, she would swear that Sharif was much like her sons in appearance…

She straightened. ''What must be done, will be done. Tell Kadar that he should return home at once. Prolonging his stay will do nothing but endanger him, and I am positive that is the last thing Serena would want.''

Tears jumped into her eyes, unanticipated, so Rose turned away. She flipped on the television to deflect her family's attention from her—and halted. There on the screen was Serena, in a picture taken at The Desert Rose, wearing the apron she had been so fond of wearing.

The news anchor stated that a band of renegade bandits from Sorajhee had lit several fires along the border of Balahar—a sign that trouble there was worsening. Rose clasped her hands together, her lips pressed tight. As a former queen, she knew exactly what those burning fires undeniably meant.

Serena would have no choice but to quench the blaze—by marrying a man she could never love.

"I'M RETURNING HOME," Cade told his co-pilot, who was staying in the hotel room next door. "I'll be ready to leave in an hour." He hung up the phone, his heart heavy.

Serena had been quite adamant that she would not see him, nor return with him. He'd been prepared to wait around until he could change her mind; he wanted so badly for her to understand that he'd come to feel about her something he'd never expected.

But her voice had been cool, her words cold. He had heard the purpose in her words to him.

She would do her duty.

Which really shouldn't surprise him. She had done her duty when she'd married him—and been completely up-front about her reasons for leaving the country with him and not exposing his identity.

Oh, no. Serena had been all about her family and her country from the start.

He just hadn't wanted to acknowledge that there was something out there more important to her than him.

A knock on the door sounded. "I like co-pilots who can be ready to fly on a moment's notice," Cade muttered, getting up to answer it.

The tall man outside was a stranger to him. "Can I help you?" he asked.

The man glanced in both directions in the hall before asking, "I am Abdul-Rahim. If I may come in, I would like to speak to you on a matter of some urgency concerning the Princess Serena."

Chapter Eighteen

"Queen Layla has orchestrated the problems behind the situation that has brought Princess Serena home," Abdul-Rahim explained. "Upon discovering that you and the princess had not consummated the royal marriage, she realized there was still a chance for her to marry one of her own into the palace."

Cade cocked a brow at the nervous man. "Why are you telling me this now?"

"Because I do not feel it is in the best interests of my king to give his daughter to Prince Ali Denarif, which he is on the verge of doing. Indeed, he must, to quiet the storm Layla has been stirring in Sorajhee against King Zakariyya."

"And so what do you expect me to do?" Cade wasn't certain if he could trust the advice of a man who appeared like a rabbit out of a hat. He wasn't about to jump into a national problem he barely understood.

"You must consummate your marriage to the Princess Serena, in order that the marriage remains valid," Abdul-Rahim explained.

Cade stared at him. "Right. There are a few things standing in the way of that happening, friend. Mainly, she's just told me to shove off. Second, I couldn't get into the palace if I wanted. Third, it goes against my grain to do something just to thwart someone, this Layla person. In other words, I'm not going to make love to a woman just to brand her."

Abdul-Rahim was shocked. "For what other reason does a man make love to his wife, then?"

Raising his brows, Cade said, "We may be suffering a bit of culture clash."

"I do not understand. If you want to stay married to Serena, why will you not do this thing? Do you not find her desirable?"

"Yes," Cade growled, not wanting Serena's desirability discussed like the weather. "If she doesn't love me, though, I'm not going to stampede into the palace and haul my wife off like a steer."

"Perhaps I am not using the proper words," Abdul-Rahim apologized. "I am only wishing to do what is best for my king. Having Layla nearer the throne does not suit me, Prince Kadar. Although she believes I am loyal to her and Azzam, King Zak is my sovereign."

Cade started at the sound of his royal title. "Call me Cade. It is who I am."

''You are Prince Kadar, son of Ibrahim, and right now, it is best for you to remember that fact,'' the adviser said stubbornly. ''It was dangerous for me to come here. I do not have time to explain your royal duty to you.''

''I don't do duty to crowns and thrones.''

''Then do it for family,'' Abdul-Rahim snapped. ''Princess Serena would be completely unhappy with Ali Denarif, as unhappy as your mother ever was by what was done to her by Queen Layla's hand.''

Cade's blood went cold.

''So I have finally got your attention.'' He walked over to the table, where grapes and bananas were arranged in an ornamental bowl. Picking some grapes, he carefully said, ''You do not know Prince Ali Denarif. He is not a good person. He would not make a good ruler.''

''That's not my concern.''

''It is your concern!'' Abdul-Rahim thundered. He tossed the grapes back into the bowl and stared at Cade sternly. ''What was the life of your father to you that you would so carelessly say you don't do duty to crowns and thrones, that you have no concerns here? Was your father's life nothing to you?''

''I wasn't old enough—''

''You are now. You are old enough,'' Abdul-Rahim said quietly. ''You must be man enough to assist the countries your father felt strongly about. And you must be prince enough to keep your wife yours.''

Cade exhaled, his emotions torn. For years he had been hidden, kept from the light of destiny. Now it was blazing on him like an inescapable inferno. ''What the hell, exactly, do you think I should do?''

Abdul-Rahim smiled thinly, his eyes shining with triumph. ''I think you should take your case to the people. Let them choose between you and Ali Denarif.''

Cade snorted. ''They will not choose me. They do not know me.''

''They know Ali Denarif the Cruel.''

Cade felt the blood drain from his head. ''What are you saying?''

The adviser raised an eyebrow. ''He is cruel and has earned the name by the people.''

''Cruel to whom?''

''What difference? Servants. Animals. Why does that concern you?''

''Women?'' Cade's heart raced painfully in his chest.

''Oh, women.'' Abdul-Rahim snapped his fingers dismissively. ''He does not like women at all.''

''I don't believe King Zak would consent for his daughter to marry a man who would hurt her.''

''Ali Denarif will not hurt Serena physically. But neither will he show her the accord of favored wife.

She will be ignored except for when he must have her at state functions.''

"Then how will his marriage to Serena be consummated? It wouldn't be any more a real marriage than when she was with me.''

"Oh. Well, he will force himself once, you see. Determination for a throne runs strong in most men. They will do anything, including a sex act that they are not used to performing.''

"I've got the picture in Technicolor,'' Cade said stonily. "Tell me exactly how you suggest I throw myself on the will of the people.''

IT WAS EVENING, and Serena's heart was heavy. All day she had dreaded this moment. Tonight, at a Balahar-Sorajhee festival celebrated by royals and non-royals alike, her father would most likely make the announcement concerning her official engagement to Ali Denarif. There would be no turning back once those words were spoken.

Serena shivered, wishing she could magically stop the clock on the mantel. The delicate hands ticked omnipresently onward. She wrapped her white silk shawl more closely to her, though she didn't need warmth on this summer evening. Her shoes were square-heeled gold sandals; she had chosen an Arabian fooston of white and gold with elaborate golden beadwork, and a gold circlet holding a light veil over her hair. Rather than hide herself in the shame she knew other people thought she should feel, she chose to hold her head high, dressing accordingly.

The marriage annulment had turned out to be a non-event. Cade's agreement had not even been required; Serena was fairly certain that his acquiescence was a foregone conclusion since the marriage had never been consummated.

To be certain of her pure state, she'd undergone a humiliating appointment with the palace physician. The memory still made her wince.

Yet after enjoying the freedom she'd experienced in the United States, she told herself she could be happy in Balahar again. There was much work here still to be done, work only a female could do.

She could serve her country better here than married to Kadar and living on The Desert Rose.

Her eyelashes lowered. She didn't feel very princesslike to wish she could have had a happily-ever-after in Texas. Nothing in her life would ever make her feel the way she'd felt with Kadar—wanted, for herself.

Pushing the thought from her mind, she slipped her fingers behind a light curtain and peered at the crowd of hundreds gathering outside of the palace. This festival was one of the people's favorite events of the year. A nonreligious holiday, it was mainly a chance for people of Balahar and Sorajhee alike to mingle on the palace grounds. Tiny lights sparkled all through the trees, lending a magical glow to the balmy night.

She sighed, and let the curtain fall back into place as a knock sounded at the door. "Yes?"

Her father came inside. "You are ready, daughter?"

"I am."

He held out his arm for her to take, which she did. "You are beautiful."

"Thank you, Father." But she couldn't smile at the compliment.

"You seem…pensive tonight. Are you unhappy to be back at the palace?" he asked, his tone worried.

"No, Father," she said softly. She thought about the fires that burned on the border between Sorajhee and Balahar and held her head high. "I pray we will all be happy tonight. This festival comes at the best possible time to generate goodwill between the peoples. That is all I am thinking about."

He patted her hand. "You are more queen than you realize, Serena. I am proud of you."

Sharif joined them, kissing his sister on the cheek, and the three of them went out to stand on the marble patio overlooking the lawns. Ali Denarif no doubt would soon join them.

And then she would force herself to be the blossoming queen her father believed her to be.

PEOPLE THRONGED the sides of the patio, standing toe-to-toe on the lawns to peer at their king and his children. Serena smiled to herself as her father raised a hand to salute his people. Off to the side, Prince Ali Denarif and a royal entourage marched in and stepped onto the marble near the king. Serena's breath caught in her throat.

Then her breath nearly died as a hush fell over the people. Rather than the cheering that usually erupted when a royal personage appeared, it was as if they silently voiced their disapproval.

This is all wrong, Serena thought wildly. *The people do not want Prince Ali Denarif—and neither do I!*

THE UNCOMFORTABLE SILENCE that came over the crowd was the spur Cade needed to vault out of hiding and jump the short, marble enclosure, landing neatly in between Serena and Ali Denarif. A gasp went up from the crowd; Ali Denarif's people drew their decorative swords; Sharif grinned, and Serena's eyes went wide as she stared at him.

And that, Cade thought, was coming to rescue the princess with a bang—Texas-style. "What do you think about the duds?" he asked.

She eyed his headdress of white *gutrah* and black-banded *agal,* and black formal suit with approval. "You look like the sheikh prince I always dreamed of for myself."

He winked at her. "I am." Turning, he faced the crowd.

"I am Prince Kadar Coleman-El Jeved," he announced loudly. "Son of Ibrahim Bin Habib El Jeved, grandson of King Habib Bin Mohammed El Jeved of Sorajhee." He held up his hand to show the ring with the royal crest of Sorajhee as the citizens erupted with shrieking and clapping. He waved them to silence. "I wish to wed with the Princess Serena, but so does Prince Ali Denarif. I throw myself on the mercy of the people to accept me as part of their family. I ask this most humbly, because I love Princess Serena, and I believe she loves me."

Clapping, chanting and crying rent the air, and flowers were thrown onto the marble. Ali Denarif kicked away the flowers that landed nearest him.

"You cannot do this," he told Kadar. "You are an imposter who has the king under his spell. Everyone knows the princes of El Jeved died in childhood."

"Actually, every one of us lives," Cade said quietly, his voice tinged with warning. "Do not use that tone with me again," he commanded.

Ali Denarif stiffened but said not another word.

"Kadar," Princess Serena said, her fingers lightly touching the ends of his headdress. "What are you doing?"

"I am begging the people to allow me to keep

the woman I love,'' he said huskily. The cheering and chanting grew louder as the crowd realized something special was happening. They remembered Ibrahim, and they felt it an honor to welcome home a favored son from the dead, a miracle no one imagined to witness. "I am asking you to keep me, Serena. Stay with me. Be my wife. Bear my princes and princesses. Most of all, love me.''

She twined her fingers into his as they gazed into each other's eyes. The people clapped, stomping the ground to show their approval, and neither she nor Kadar noticed that Ali Denarif left in disgust, nor that her father nodded his happy benediction of their love.

"Yes,'' Serena said, her voice holding all the joy he wanted to hear her speak. "I will love you, and marry you, and hopefully, one day bear children as wise and brave as their father.''

It might not have been tradition, but Kadar had handled all the royal details he could for one night. He had his wife in his arms for good and he kissed her long and gratefully, a man who suddenly knew exactly what it felt like to win the woman of his dreams.

Epilogue

"At last I have you exactly where I want you," Serena teased her prince as they lay in each other's arms in the marriage bed. Beneath hanging velvet swags and enclosed by curtains, they'd made love, falling in love with each other a little more with this new bonding between them.

"At last I have *you* exactly where I want *you,*" Cade echoed, rolling over so that he could kiss Serena. "I've dreamed of this for so long I feel I'm living an Arabian tale."

Serena laughed softly. "I thought perhaps you never spent a night sleepless for desiring me."

"Oh, I spent those," he said with a growl, nipping at her neck. "And days, too."

"That's all over now, my husband proper." She wound her arms around his neck and pulled him close.

"No," he said, before his lips closed over hers,

"the honeymoon begins right now—and whether we're in Texas or Balahar, it never ends."

IN TEXAS, happy tears jumped into Rose's eyes as she saw the television replay the moment her son raised his hand high to reveal the royal crest, saw the highly unorthodox kiss her son laid on his princess. With gratitude, she heard the people cheer, saw the smile on King Zak's face.

She'd cried out so loudly upon seeing Cade on TV that everyone in the kitchen had run into the room to see what was happening. Alex high-fived Mac, and Jessica grinned.

"Well, Mac," Jessica said, "I guess that ended with the right prince getting the right woman after all."

Mac raised a brow at his cousin. "I said in the beginning that I wasn't getting married, didn't I? I'm always right."

Jessica smirked at her cousin. "You won't always be such a renegade," she warned, her grin knowing. "Two princes down...it's turning into a real wedding rodeo around here."

She sighed with dramatic abandon, and the men in the room rolled their eyes. Ignoring their teasing, she perked up, all thoughts of weddings leaving her mind. "By the way, did I tell you all that my friend, Abbie, is staying with us for the summer? She says

she's got something important to tell me—and I
can't wait to hear!''

Don't miss

HIS SHOTGUN PROPOSAL

*by Karen Toller Whittenburg,
on sale in June 2001
from Harlequin American Romance,
to find out what happens next in*

TEXAS SHEIKHS!

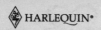

Meet 50 loving dads in

babies
& BACHELORS USA

Take 4 FREE BOOKS,
Plus get a FREE GIFT!

Babies & Bachelors USA is a heartwarming new collection of reissued novels featuring 50 sexy heroes from every state who experience the ups and downs of fatherhood and find time for love all the same. All of the books, hand-picked by our editors, are outstanding romances by some of the world's bestselling authors, including Stella Bagwell, Kristine Rolofson, Judith Arnold and Marie Ferrarella!

Don't delay, order today! Call customer service at
1-800-873-8635.
Or
Clip this page and mail to The Reader Service:

In U.S.A.
P.O. Box 9049
Buffalo, NY
14269-9049

In CANADA
P.O. Box 616
Fort Erie, Ontario
L2A 5X3

YES! Please send me four FREE BOOKS and FREE GIFT along with the next four novels on a 14-day free home preview. If I like the books and decide to keep them, I'll pay just $15.96* U.S. or $18.00* CAN., and there's no charge for shipping and handling. Otherwise, I'll keep the 4 FREE BOOKS and FREE GIFT and return the rest. If I decide to continue, I'll receive six books each month—two of which are always free—until I've received the entire collection. In other words, if I collect all 50 volumes, I will have paid for 32 and received 18 absolutely free!

267 HCK 4537
467 HCK 4538

Name	(Please Print)		
Address			Apt. #
City		State/Prov.	Zip/Postal Code

*Terms and prices subject to change without notice.
  Sales Tax applicable in N.Y. Canadian residents will be charged applicable provincial taxes
  and GST. All orders are subject to approval.

DIRBAB02

© 2000 Harlequin Enterprises Limited

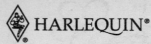

Harlequin invites you to walk down the aisle...

To honor our year long celebration of weddings, we are offering an exciting opportunity for you to own the Harlequin Bride Doll. Handcrafted in fine bisque porcelain, the wedding doll is dressed for her wedding day in a cream satin gown accented by lace trim. She carries an exquisite traditional bridal bouquet and wears a cathedral-length dotted Swiss veil. Embroidered flowers cascade down her lace overskirt to the scalloped hemline; underneath all is a multi-layered crinoline.

Join us in our celebration of weddings by sending away for your own Harlequin Bride Doll. This doll regularly retails for $74.95 U.S./approx. $108.68 CDN. One doll per household. Requests must be received no later than June 30, 2001. Offer good while quantities of gifts last. Please allow 6-8 weeks for delivery. Offer good in the U.S. and Canada only. Become part of this exciting offer!

Simply complete the order form and mail to:
"A Walk Down the Aisle"

IN U.S.A	IN CANADA
P.O. Box 9057	P.O. Box 622
3010 Walden Ave.	Fort Erie, Ontario
Buffalo, NY 14240-9057	L2A 5X3

Enclosed are eight (8) proofs of purchase found on the last page of every specially marked Harlequin series book and $3.75 check or money order (for postage and handling). Please send my Harlequin Bride Doll to:

_____
Name (PLEASE PRINT)

_____
Address   Apt. #

_____
City   State/Prov.   Zip/Postal Code

_____
Account # (if applicable)   **098 KIK DAEW**

HARLEQUIN®
Makes any time special®

Visit us at www.eHarlequin.com

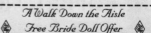

A Walk Down the Aisle
Free Bride Doll Offer
One Proof-of-Purchase

PHWDAPOP